TRAPPED!

The boys were caught in a cave after an earthquake sealed off the only entrance with a sheet of solid rock.

It all began when Ron and Edward decided to hunt for the lost pirate treasure in the cave in Squaw Mountain. They were disgusted to discover a tagalong—Edward's kid brother Scotty. Little did they know that their lives might well depend on the packrat tendencies of the younger boy.

Just when the three thought they'd escaped, they found themselves on the Squaw's Nose, a large shelf on the mountainside guarded by sheer cliffs. The only way off was back through the now-blocked cave!

CHOICE BOOKS
THE BEST IN FAMILY READING
P. O. Box 706
Goshen, IN 46526
We Welcome Your Response

TREASURE ON SQUAW MOUNTAIN

Marjorie Zimmerman

David C. Cook Publishing Co.

ELGIN, ILLINOIS—WESTON, ONTARIO
LA HABRA, CALIFORNIA

TREASURE ON SQUAW MOUNTAIN

David C. Cook Publishing Co., Elgin, IL 60120

First printing, August, 1976
Second printing, December, 1976
Third printing, March, 1977

Printed in the United States of America
Library of Congress Catalog Number: 75-36696
ISBN: 0-912692-85-5

For Jason, Joshua
and Sarah Ruth

CONTENTS

1

Tales of Buried Treasure

EDWARD JOGGED OVER THE HARD-PACKED SAND of Musket Beach toward the log shelter. It was a neat July day. The surf boomed and the sea gulls swooped and dipped, screaming in their raucous voices. To think that back in Cleveland he had dug in his heels against this Oregon vacation.

He reached the shelter and ducked behind it. Ron Devlin was already there. "Beats me," he snorted as Edward flopped down beside him. "Let me have a day off, and what do I get? Wind and fog every time. Can't fish, swim or surf." The 16-year-old giant, who had a part-time job at the supermarket, swiped at the gritty particles which the wind hurled against his face.

Edward digested his complaint in silence. Maybe it wasn't such a great day after all. You couldn't play Frisbee in a gusty wind, and the sand blew into your eyes and mouth when you opened them. "And me with only four days left."

Ron looked unhappy. "You headed back home Saturday?"

Edward nodded and kicked a foot viciously into the loose sand. "Ow!" He bounced upright to nurse a bruised toe. "I must have hit a land mine." He leaned over and dug in the sand. "Ha! That is a most interesting-looking rock." He hefted the offending object in his hand: coffee-colored, smooth as marble, and feather-light.

Ron looked over his shoulder at it. "Interesting-looking, maybe; rock, no. That's beeswax, pal. It's probably 300 years old."

"What's it doing here?"

Ron reached for it and turned it over in his hand. "Washed up from a shipwreck. If you'd been lucky you'd have stubbed your toe on a Spanish doubloon or a gold ornament. A pirate ship was lost on this part of the coast in 1703."

"Pirates yet!"

Ron's slow grin showed white on his bronzed face. "You wouldn't be interested in the treasure they hid on Squaw Mountain; that's only Indian legend. The shipwreck is a fact, though."

Edward yawned. "Let the whole thing hang out."

Ron, who was a walking encyclopedia about this part of the Oregon coast, told how a Spanish vessel (a "canoe with wings"), which had been seized by pirates for her rich cargo, was lost on the Point, spilling the contents of her hold all over the beach. Beeswax, gold coins, crucifixes and jeweled ornaments continued to be dug out of the sand for many years after the ship went down, but the real treasure had been hidden in a mountain cave, or so ran the Nehalem legend. This treasure had never been discovered.

In spite of Edward's skepticism he shivered as Ron's laconic sentences raised sharp images in his mind. He saw the Spanish galleon floundering in a terrific gale; heard the groaning of the canvas, and the jibs cracking like gunshots as the ship shuddered convulsively.

He saw the mean-faced pirates racing across the slippery, slanting decks as the ship heeled over in the storm. They lowered the treasure chest over the side, swarmed after it, and somehow made it through heavy seas to the beach.

Indians peered out from the shelter of the woods as the swarthy seamen built a fire of driftwood to dry their dripping garments and then, cutlasses at their sides, flung themselves down on the damp sand for a few hours of fitful sleep. They awoke in the dismal foggy dawn, cursing and wretched, seized an unwary young Nehalem brave and forced him to shoulder the chest up the mountainside. Near the summit they hid the treasure in a cave, killed the Indian, then struck off down the coast and vanished forever.

His dreaming eyes slowly focused. "It's a great story, but it's as full of holes as a fishnet."

"Yeah? Like what?"

"You say yourself they polished off the only witness up there on the mountain."

"All right, Perry Mason. The young brave's girl friend had secretly followed them up the trail and saw the whole thing. She hotfooted it back to the tribe and spilled the story, probably hoping for revenge. But the Nehalems are peaceable, and they were probably superstitious about the murder, since they thought the spirits lived in the mountaintops, so they never went inside the cave. Satisfied?"

"You have allayed some of my doubts. But still—have you ever been inside the cave?"

"Sure, lots of times. I guided some summer people up there last year. But I'll be a flea's left eyebrow if anybody ever digs up any treasure in Pirates' Cave."

"Why?"

Ron shrugged. "Solid rock floor, rock walls. No place for a beetle to hide."

"You sure you have the right cave?" Edward inquired.

"I'm sure. There are some rocks with funny marks on them that identify it. No one's ever been able to decode the hieroglyphics, though."

OK, forget the treasure, thought Edward, it's the cave I'm interested in. Ever since he'd read

Alonzo Pond's book on caverns he'd been itching to do some spelunking—cave exploring. His mild acrophobia wouldn't bother him in a cave, and if it showed up in climbing a low mountain like Squaw, that would give him the opportunity to overcome it, wouldn't it?

He looked up at Ron. "What are the possibilities of an excursion to this legendary site, even this very day? Within the hour, in fact."

Ron sorted out the words. "You want to go up to Pirates' Cave right now? Good idea."

Edward had counted on this reaction. He hadn't known Ron long, but long enough to know something of his interests.

"Matter of fact," Ron went on, "this is the best kind of day for a mountain climb. Won't be too hot. If we get going right away we can be back by dinner time."

"Great. I'll go along!" said a voice from above them.

They turned and looked up. The pudgy boy stretched out on the bank, with his blond hair hanging over the edge, had the same bright blue eyes as Edward.

"Eavesdropping again, punk?"

"This is a free country. I just happen to be watching for whales. Anyway, I can go to the cave with you and Ron, can't I?"

"Why would we want you tagging along?" Edward spoke reasonably. "You are laboring under a

13

delusion, sonny, if you think mountain climbing is for little kids."

"You're only three years older than I am, Edward McKee!" yelled the infuriated 11-year-old. "I weigh just as much as you do. Besides, I'm real good at cracking codes. Remember that book on ciphers I got for Christmas? I could read those Egyptian words for you."

Edward sighed. "Scotty, my boy, you are full of hallucinations."

"I could carry your gear," he said stubbornly, "like the shepherds do in the Himalayas."

"Sherpas, punk. But you're so accident-prone that Mom would never let you climb a mountain."

The truth of that silenced Scotty for a moment, and Edward jumped to his feet. "Come on, Ron, let's tell my mother and get rolling."

Scotty trailed after them up to the summer cottage, where they burst into the kitchen as Mrs. McKee was washing the breakfast dishes.

2

Tomahawk Trail

EDWARD'S MOM LISTENED to his plan to climb Squaw Mountain with Ron and explore Pirates' Cave with the uncertain expression she always wore when either of her sons planned some activity.

"Climb a mountain? Mercy, Edward, you've never climbed a mountain in your life. I don't know what your father would say."

"Squaw Mountain isn't a real honest-to-goodness mountain, Mrs. McKee," Ron put in hastily. "There aren't any ice caps or snowfields, nothing like that. If you stay on the trail you aren't in any danger."

They all glanced out the window at the blunt, green-mantled mountain across the highway as he spoke. A ledge, dubbed "The Squaw's Nose," projected at right angles from its north side, giving the mountain the comical appearance of a profile with a big humped nose. From this distance the mountain appeared to be an elevation of easy ascents and gentle slopes, disappointingly free of hazards, in fact.

"We want to take our lunch up to the cave, Mom. Ron says we can climb it easily in three hours, and we'd be back before sundown." Edward gave her his most winning smile.

"Tomahawk Trail is as safe as a church," Ron emphasized. "We wouldn't be going close to the ridge or near any cliffs."

"But it would be windy up there. You'd have to dress warmly. Remember your allergies, Edward."

"I'll wear my windbreaker."

His mother still looked dissatisfied. "We came to Musket Beach to attend the Bible conference, and you've already missed several meetings."

He tried to keep the impatience out of his voice. "I can go to church at home, Mom, but I can't climb a mountain in Cleveland. I'll go to the evening service with you, I promise."

She sighed. "Well, I suppose it's all right. I know you've grown up in this area, Ron, and I've heard you're an excellent woodsman. But you put a sweater on under your windbreaker, Edward."

"Hey, Mom, I want to go with them," Scotty clamored. "You heard what Ron said. Tomahawk Trail is as safe as a church. I want to go too, Mom."

His mother laughed. "I'd as soon let you climb a

16

mountain, Scotty, as put your head in a lion's mouth."

"Aw, for crying out loud!"

"Absolutely not, Scotty. You'd fall off a precipice or get lost before you'd been out half an hour."

You'd think Squaw Mountain was the Matterhorn to hear his mother sputtering, Edward thought. He realized she was picturing her younger son dangling against a cliff with an ice ax between his teeth. But though he felt sorry for poor Scotty, he knew she'd made the right decision. Accidents that were on their way to happen to other people pounced on Scotty.

Ron went home to get ready, and Edward rapidly changed his clothes before his mother could change her mind. He'd held his breath when she fussed about his missing the morning meeting. He knew she was unhappy about his lack of interest in the Bible conference, but she needn't have been. He believed the same things she and Dad did, but who would choose to be shut up inside while adventure called so loudly? Time enough for church when they got back home.

He put on the smothering clothing his mother had insisted on, and congratulated himself that he'd packed his hiking boots when they left home. When he got back to the kitchen, his mother had sandwiches and a thermos of orange juice ready. However much she sputtered, she usually came through in the end.

17

At the door he turned to Scotty, who sat with his legs draped over the arm of his chair, gazing moodily out at the mountain. "Sorry, bud. Maybe next summer, if we come back."

"Aw, I don't really care about seeing that dumb old cave."

"I'll copy the code and bring it back for you. If you can break it, the treasure might pay our dentist bill."

Scotty's grunt was noncommittal. "Where does that stupid Tomahawk Trail start, anyway?" he asked indifferently as Edward ran down the steps.

"Across the highway, Ron said, at that little picnic grounds."

Ron, waiting at the end of the lane, looked taller than usual in his jeans, jacket and billed cap. He carried a second hat in his hand which he clapped on Edward's head. "It's an old one. If the sun breaks out later we'll need protection."

Edward settled the hat on his head while Ron stowed the lunch in his rucksack. He eyed Ron's pack. "You resemble a donkey about to cross the Andes."

"Survival items. It's not smart to trail hike without a compass and matches and a knife. I carry a small hatchet too, and we'll need the flashlight in the cave. Add a first-aid kit and our lunches—" He shrugged.

They crossed the highway and struck out over the fields, where a brisk wind was flattening the tall, tough grasses like an oncoming ocean wave.

"The trail doesn't go near the Nose." Ron followed Edward's gaze. "We go up the other side. Some people think the Indians used to offer human sacrifices on the Nose, but they couldn't have. You can't get to that ledge from above or below either. It just sticks out there like a shelf, sheer cliff above and more of the same below."

"A desert island in midair." Edward was intrigued.

They entered the woods and Ron led the way on a spongy trail that took them up a gentle slope. Edward drew the evergreen-scented air deep into his lungs, and promptly sneezed. His stupid allergy!

"What's your theory about the treasure, Ron?" he asked as he climbed over a fallen log. "Did the Indians make up the story?"

"Why would they? Besides, if there's no truth in a story it generally dies out after a couple of generations."

"But what happened to the treasure? The news would have been out if anyone had discovered it."

"Seems so."

"Couldn't it still be there? The cave may have altered its formation through the years. Live caves do, if there's running water and limestone deposits."

"There's nothing 'live' about Pirates' Cave," Ron said reluctantly. "It's a dusty little place with a few spiders running around."

"Dust and spiders." Edward resettled his hat. "I was holding out for a stalactite or two, or a limestone drapery. Never mind, I don't really care. This trail makes up for everything."

He had never dreamed the mountain could be such a paradise. The July sun filtered down between the firs, making puddles of light and shadow around the dark trunks. Ferns gushed up among the rocks like fountains, and the glossy, crinkly edged leaves of the Oregon grape clutched at their clothes as they pushed past them.

The trail carried them over fallen logs velvety with moss and through clumps of salal bushes brilliant with frosty blue berries.

"And we took all this away from the Indians." Edward wagged his head. "Manifest destiny, we called it. No wonder they regard us with something less than enthusiasm."

The trail grew steeper, and the sun shone hotly on them as the trees gradually thinned out.

Edward pushed his cap back on his forehead. "My mom missed the boat when she required me to don a thick jacket and a sweltering sweater. These clothes will be the death of me yet."

Ron said consolingly, "You may be glad for that jacket before we get back. Never can tell."

They fell silent, saving their breath as the climb grew steeper. Edward admired the way Ron moved steadily ahead, never hurrying, never lagging. And no sign of fatigue in his hard-muscled body.

20

After a while the sun went under a cloud, but the atmosphere grew no cooler; in fact, it was now decidedly sultry. Just about the time when Edward was wishing heartily for a breather, Ron slowed his pace to study the terrain. They were both thirsty, and took time for a drink of orange juice from Edward's thermos.

Edward recapped the bottle. "Are we almost there?"

"Yup."

He felt a quiet elation. He was chicken about heights, but so far no one knew it but himself.

The air was uncomfortably humid, and he had stopped to take off his jacket when he heard a sharp exclamation from Ron. The other boy had gained the slope. "Hey! Something's happened up here. Look at this!"

Edward dug his toes into the trail and panted to the top. Then he stood there, gaping.

Before them a tree lay uprooted, its great gnarled roots upturned to the sky. Beneath it the mountainside was split open like a cracked melon, and the tree lay across the chasm, forming a natural bridge. Edward's eyes were drawn hypnotically to the cut plunging deep into the heart of the mountain, but he tore them away at Ron's question. "See the knoll?" He was pointing across the chasm.

Edward picked out the little hill flanked by twin pines and the rock formation at the cave site.

21

"That tree fell just right for us," Ron pointed out with satisfaction. "We can't get across on that side." He jerked a thumb to the left, and Edward saw a series of descending rocky ledges. "And if we detoured around on *that* side it would take us way off course." He swung his long legs up onto the log and began squirming forward on his belly.

There was a low snarl of thunder, and he looked over his shoulder at his motionless friend. "Better get cracking."

"Ah, yes, forward march, on our stomachs as an army marches." With a prayer that he wouldn't vomit, Edward clawed his way onto the big trunk. Gripping the rough bark with his sweating hands, he inched forward, fixing his eyes on the opposite end. Incredibly, as he moved his nausea lifted. Then Ron jumped down and Edward followed him.

Dizzy now with joy, he sprinted after Ron in the direction of the knoll.

3

Scotty Sets Out

SCOTTY STRADDLED THE PORCH RAILING and watched his brother lope up the lane to join Ron Devlin. Edward looked pretty sharp in his red windbreaker, with the blue turtleneck his mother had insisted on. And there was a T-shirt under that, Scotty guessed. He grinned wickedly. Edward would cook to death climbing the trail under a hot sun in that outfit, but there wasn't much you could do about Mom.

The pair struck off across the highway and over the fields without so much as a backward glance, and Scotty wandered back into the cottage.

"We'll go over to Seacrest after the morning meeting," said his mother cheerfully, "and you can have one of those monstrous chocolate sundaes with whipped cream and cherries that you like so much."

But Scotty shook his head. "Sounds neat, Mom, but Tim Gesswein wants me to spend the day over there. I'll take my lunch. Can I, Mom? I'll fix my own sandwiches. We're going to build a fort."

"But you'll miss the youth meeting again."

"Aw, Mom," he whined, "just this once, please."

By now his mother was wearing the expression of combat fatigue which their conversations so often produced. "Oh, all right. But stay on the Gessweins' beach and be sure you get home before four o'clock."

Scotty made a dive for the kitchen and went to work on his lunch before she could change her mind.

"You're taking enough food to feed an army." His mother eyed his stocky frame as he stuffed a paper bag with peanut butter sandwiches, bananas, an orange, several hard-boiled eggs he found in a bowl, a large hunk of cheese, and some brownies. After she left the room he added another sandwich, a big piece of chocolate cake, a fistful of raisins, and a package of hot dogs from the refrigerator.

"Gotta have plenty to eat." He managed to conceal the second bag as she came back into the kitchen. "You know Tim."

"I know *you*." Against her better judgment she slipped some chocolate bars into his bag. Then she looked him over. "Hm! I don't expect you to be a clothes horse, but that ragged old jacket looks disgraceful enough without the safety pin on the pocket."

"Oh, I've gotta have that, the zipper's broken on that pocket. Sure, I'll be careful. Nope, I won't forget, I'll stay close to their cottage. So long, Mom."

He grabbed his lunch bags and scooted out the door before she could ask him what the queer lump was at his waistline. If he were as tall as Ron he could conceal a pick in the leg of his jeans, but he had to content himself with a hammer, and it clanked coldly against his stomach as he scrambled down the weedy bank and headed up the beach in the direction of Tim's house.

As soon as he was out of sight of the cottage he crouched down behind a log to transfer his rations from the bags to his many pockets. A couple of them were already loaded, but he'd need the slingshot on the way up the mountain; the wad of nylon cord he'd found on the beach yesterday might come in handy for hauling the treasure chest home. Even a knife with a broken blade was good for some things, and the dried starfish was neat. The candle stubs were probably a dumb idea and he considered dumping them, then thought better of it.

He had picked this old jacket for its many huge pockets, and every one of them bulged and flopped as he loped toward the cove.

He squirmed a little when he thought of the way

he had deceived Mom, but in a way it was her own fault. She always heard different words than the ones he said. If you said "swim" to Mom she heard "drown"; if you said "climb" she heard "break your neck."

At the cove, wet ropes of seaweed garlanded some glistening black rocks, and near them a crab scuttled into a rock pool. He leaped over the shallow stream which flowed sluggishly across the sand, and trotted up the bank to the highway, dashing across it with his head pulled into his jacket collar like a turtle and his baseball cap yanked down over his eyes.

A worry nagged at him. What if the trail in the woods was so faint that a city kid wouldn't be able to spot it?

But his worries were over when he entered the woods, where he saw the well-marked trail which the pirates had climbed long ago. At the thought, he became a brave and prowled along the brown-needled trail, aiming his hammer now and then at a thorny bush and trying to imitate the calls of the birds. When the trail grew so steep it made him puff, he stopped to pick some berries while a squirrel scolded him from a stump. There were other voices, too. You might think a mountain was a silent place, but if you listened you could hear the stealthy scurryings of small animals, the whir of wings from a thicket, the scratchy rustle of leaves in the underbrush. His slingshot was in his pocket but it hardly seemed fair to use it here—this was *their* territory in a special kind of way.

He went on, his path winding among some blackened tree stubs and past blackberry vines which clawed at his bulging pockets and slashed his wrists.

The sun, rising higher, brought out the beads of sweat on his upper lip, and he wished he had brought a thermos bottle. Maybe there was a stream nearby. He pushed his old cap back on his head and stood listening for the sound of water. He didn't hear that but he did notice, beyond the undergrowth off to the left, a rise high enough to provide a view. Probably old Chief Galloping Horse used to stand there and look down at the smoke of his village. Say, it would be fun to pick out the McKee cottage and Tim's house from that height.

He turned from the trail, pushed through the brush, and clambered over rocks and logs, his pockets flopping heavily. It was farther than it had looked. Skirting the ridge, he scrambled up a sharp incline and gained the summit.

He was standing on a hogback, and the silver ocean surged far below. He saw the crescent of golden sand which was Musket Beach, the cottages looking like toy houses, and the figures which resembled dolls. He gazed delightedly at the scene, wishing he'd brought the binoculars, so that he could get a clearer view of everything. Well, better

27

not stand here all day, Scotty thought to himself.

He turned, stubbed his toe on a protruding root, and without warning went head over heels down the slope. He was dizzily aware as he hurtled downward of the nothingness beyond the ridge.

4

A Smelly Encounter

AS SCOTTY CRASHED DOWN THE SLOPE toward the rim of the canyon, his flailing hands grasped in vain at tough grass, rank weeds, anything that might avert disaster. But the scrubby brush was shallow-rooted and came away in his hands.

In the nick of time he thrust out a foot and braked himself against a sapling in his path. He sat up and took a deep breath. Wow! His mother hadn't been kidding when she made that remark about falling off a cliff. He'd skinned his knee and worse, mashed his lunch. "You won't catch me leaving the trail again," he vowed aloud as he picked up his hammer and retraced his steps.

And now the trail twisted and ascended in earnest. He pressed through dense thickets which slashed cheek and hands, chopping at them with his hammer as he struggled along.

On a switchback where the sun blazed hotly, he stopped to slip his arms out of his jacket and tie the sleeves around his waist. As he did so, a movement in the brush caught his eye. He stood staring in delighted wonder. Two little furry forms with big fluffy tails were tumbling over each other in the coarse grass like a couple of kittens. He plunged toward them, itching to get his hands on the cuties, when a maternal snarl froze him.

He had been so absorbed that he hadn't given a thought to the instinct of a wild animal for its young. Too late he saw the dark form move menacingly out of the thicket toward him. The telltale white stripe down her back told the story, and Scotty leaped, tripped and rolled away.

The odor which immediately engulfed the area glued his nostrils together. Had he moved fast enough to keep from getting the smelly spray on his clothes? He thought anxiously of his lunch. Was it ruined?

He panted up the path, possessed by a burning desire to hear a human voice. He felt as if he had been alone on the trail all day, but an upward glance showed a bright sky overhead. Almost noon, he guessed. (Too bad he'd worn his watch into the swimming pool last month.)

A branch grazed his cheek. Look at the size of those berries! He was as dry as a dictionary, so he crammed some of the juicy fruit into his mouth. As he reached for a second handful he saw with some

surprise that there wasn't a broken vine or a trod-
den branch to be seen. It didn't look as if anyone
had been around here for years. The trail narrowed
too; in fact, it seemed to be going off at a tangent,
downhill.

He moved on, but the tangled brush was hard to
push through and finally became impenetrable.
He came to a puzzled halt. High boulders were
piled around him, and a spider's web, with dew-
drops still clinging to its gauze, hung in the
branches stretched across his path.

He pushed his cap far back on his head and
looked carefully around. Ho! He aimed a forefinger
at his head and uttered a sharp "Bang!" for now he
saw that he wasn't on Tomahawk Trail at all.
Dummy! In his headlong dash from the skunk family, he must have taken a wrong fork. He was on an
old deer run.

Just then the sun, as if in mourning, ducked
under a cloud. In the gloom of the forest Scotty felt
smothered—smothered by trees and brush and the
sultry atmosphere—and very much alone.

Determinedly he shook off the little chill that
crept up his backbone. Of course he wasn't lost. All
he had to do was retrace his steps to the fork and
get back on the trail. He groaned to think how far
he had fallen behind the others by this time; but,
behind or not, he was going to take a break. He was
hot and tired, and his throat felt dry enough to
crack.

He set his back against an alder and reached into his pocket for his orange. As he peeled it, it occurred to him that he could save time if, instead of going back to the fork, he could find a shortcut. In leaving Tomahawk Trail he had gone to the left, which would be east. If he now struck off west, through the underbrush and across that little gully, he would intersect Tomahawk without having that long hike back. He ate the orange slowly, enjoying the trickle of juice down his dry throat. Might be a good idea to test one of his sandwiches too, and lighten his load that much.

The sandwich tasted okay, but maybe at this stage anything would taste good. He was considering testing a brownie when there was a rustle in the brush behind him. As he turned, the stories he'd heard of people coming face to face with bears in the mountains flashed into his mind.

He sprang up, ready to strike off from the deer run toward the gully, when a little question edged into his mind. What if he somehow missed Tomahawk Trail and went round and round in circles? No one on earth would know where to look for him.

He turned and jogged back the way he'd come. The hammer seemed to weigh more all the time, and he considered discarding it but decided against it. It might mean the difference between coming away from the cave fabulously wealthy, with all those jewels and stuff, and going home empty-handed. A blow from the hammer against the key rock, and open sesame.

It wasn't hard to backtrack for he had broken trail like a herd of elephants. The Oregon grape was snapped off, torn vines dangled, and tufts of grass were trampled.

He kept his mind on what he was doing this time, and the tension went out of him when he recognized the switchback where he had sighted the skunks. He whooshed with relief when he found himself back on target, but he wouldn't be satisfied until he came within hearing of the others.

Presently he crossed a shallow, brushy canyon and when he came out of it he began seriously to study the landscape. He remembered Ron saying that the cave was in a knoll flanked by a couple of pine trees, easy to spot because almost everything up here was fir. He had to be getting close because the mountain was becoming bare and rocky, with only a few stunted trees clinging to the slopes. He had thought the air would be thin and cold this high up, but it was strangely humid and heavy.

The trail ahead of him flew upward, and he regarded it sourly until a sound, a sneeze, jolted him into action. Edward's allergy had betrayed him. They must be at the top of the slope, just out of sight.

Scotty pulled himself up the incline with the aid of some overhanging vines and then, at the top, found his way blocked by a fallen tree. Must have been hit by lightning, and when it had been up-rooted it had opened a big crack in the mountain-side.

The roots of the tree sprawled like an octopus. He clawed himself up onto the trunk, thinking sadly of his squashed lunch. He squirmed forward rapidly, noticing again how sultry it was.

He'd no more than jumped off on the other side when there was a flash of lightning and he felt a raindrop splash on his hand. He didn't mind heights and he wasn't afraid of snakes or bats, but thunder and lightning were something else. He would have to pick up the trail again fast.

The lightning zigzagged again, and at the low snarl of thunder Scotty looked wildly about him. Where were they? He swallowed hard. "Don't tell me I'm lost again."

5

Pirates' Cave

THUNDER ROARED OVER THE MOUNTAIN and rattled in the canyons as Edward dashed through the clearing at Ron's heels.

"Gotta get out from under these trees," Ron panted. The angry sky was glittering fitfully with lightning.

They made for the knoll which marked Pirates' Cave, gasping in the heavy humid air which was as smothering as a feather pillow. Those swollen black clouds would surely explode if rain didn't pour out soon to relieve the pressure. Across the clearing, the knoll, bristling with scraggly undergrowth, glowered at them menacingly. The mountain was no longer a happy place; it had become ominous.

Nothing less than the weird animallike cry Edward heard behind him could have stopped him in his tracks. He whirled. The figure blundering toward him bulged in unlikely places, gripped a hammer in one hand and a banana in the other, and was croaking, "Wait up! Wait up!" The perspiring red face under the dirty cap was imploring.

Edward whistled. "I don't believe it. . . . Hey, Ron!"

Ron turned and his jaw dropped. "You've got to be kidding. Where'd he come from?"

"I've been following you!" Scotty hollered.

As he galloped toward them, Edward's nostrils drew together. The thunder must have scared a skunk into defensive action. Then a few big raindrops hissed on the nearby rocks and he shouted, "Step on it, bud. We want to make the cave before the deluge." He leaped back and grasped Scotty's arm to drag him forward.

At the knoll, forbidding in its skull-like formation, Ron dropped to his knees near the base of a towering column of rock slabs and tore away the coarse vegetation while Edward craned his neck at the tower. The tremendous boulders were piled one on top of another as if they'd been carelessly tossed there by some giant hand. It looked as if a push would topple them, but they'd probably been balanced like that for thousands of years.

Ron uncovered a flat rock, and Edward and Scotty leaned over his shoulder to study the strange markings scratched on it. Simultaneously hail chattered on the rocks like popcorn, and Ron ducked quickly into the cave. The others crowded in on his heels, while thunder cracked overhead.

They were in a narrow tunnel which led downhill, barely allowing headroom. Ron's flashlight threw a pale flicker as daylight was blotted out behind them.

The choking cave odors of dust, moss, spiders and dead leaves mingled with a slight smell of skunk as they groped forward. Presently Ron warned, "Drop-off ahead."

Almost at once they found themselves jumping down to a rocky, uneven floor.

"The treasure room." There was laughter in Ron's voice as he flashed his light about their surroundings.

They stared wordlessly at the gray stone walls and floor, the rock ceiling—no stalagmites, stalactites, limestone formations—nothing but grim gray rock.

"For crying out loud." Scotty groped his way over to the nearest wall and tapped it with his hammer. "Solid rock," he said accusingly.

Edward stamped on the gritty floor experimentally. "Nothing less than an H-bomb would cause this floor to disintegrate," he pronounced judicially. "Is this all there is to Pirates' Cave, Ron?"

"Afraid so."

So much for the legend, then, for no treasure could have been buried beneath this floor or inserted in the walls. No matter, except that it was disappointing that the cave held no possibilities for further exploration. But he couldn't say Ron hadn't warned him.

Scotty did not accept a treasureless cave as lightly as his brother, however. "There must be a niche in the wall or something. In this TV program I saw, this guy accidentally leaned against a rock, see, and the whole wall swung open and they went into a passage—" He was moving along the wall, tapping with his hammer.

"What you see is what you get in Pirates' Cave," apologized Ron. "Say, Tiger, what kind of perfume are you using? It kind of grips a fellow."

Scotty ignored him. "What kind of a dumb cave is this, anyhow? Tom Sawyer and Becky snooped around in all kinds of passages for a week."

Edward changed the subject. "By the way, would you be so good as to tell us how you got Mom to let you come up here?"

"I dunno. I guess I whined a lot."

He should have known the punk would wangle it somehow.

Meanwhile, Ron was moving along the walls of the cave, apparently renewing acquaintance with various spider webs and dust heaps, and Edward followed him.

" 'Eye of newt and toe of frog . . . . ' " Edward's foot hit something that rattled on the stones and he jumped.

It wasn't a skull or a bloodstained blade, only a little tin pail, no doubt left behind by some disappointed spelunker.

"Here's your treasure, Scotty. This was probably full of gold and gems, but somebody got here ahead of us. And don't stand so close to me, I beg of you."

"You should have smelled me right at first. Aw, rats! Some little kid's lunch pail. Hey, you guys, why don't we eat our lunch? I'm starved!"

"Do you really yearn to dine in this black hole of Calcutta?"

The words were hardly out of Edward's mouth when there was a low, rumbling roar and the solid floor began to weave. The rocking motion was so unexpected and so severe that they all lost their balance and went sprawling in the darkness. At the same time loose rocks and rubble rained down, and they heard a tremendous thud above them.

"Earthquake!" muttered Ron after a few stunned seconds.

"Let's get out of here," Scotty squeaked.

Ron's hand was on his arm like a vise. "Don't move." His voice cracked like a whip, and he began feeling around for the flashlight. He found it and beamed it around the cave; but except for the rubble, everything looked the same.

"OK." Ron sounded relieved. "I'll go first, and don't get in a hurry, anybody."

"You know what?" Scotty babbled. "We could have been killed. We could have fallen down a crack in the earth like they did in Alaska, or the roof could have caved in. Boy, we're lucky."

Lucky was right, if that was the word. Of course, they weren't out yet. How would an earthquake affect a mountain or a forest? Uproot trees? Cause rockslides, change the course of streams, or the accessibility of trails?

The tunnel seemed endless. Presently the roof lowered. They heard Ron mutter something after they came to a halt. He seemed to be moving about, if anybody could move at all in those cramped quarters, and he grunted deeply once or twice.

"What are you doing, Ron?" Scotty asked anxiously. "Let's go. We don't care how much thunder and lightning there is, let's go."

The only sound for a moment was Ron's heavy breathing. Then he said very quietly, "Go on back to the cave."

There was something in his voice that silenced even Scotty.

6

Inside the Mountain

IN THE CAVE CHAMBER, they received Ron's frightening disclosure in characteristic ways. Edward stood absolutely silent, assessing and weighing Ron's deduction that the earthquake had obviously shaken loose a heavy boulder from the rock tower and it had fallen against the entrance, blocking it completely. Scotty instantly yelped, "You mean we're trapped in this dumb cave?"

"I couldn't budge it," Ron muttered.

"But we've got to move it, Ron," Edward said after a minute. "Otherwise . . . Come on, Ron, the two of us can do it."

"No way. Even if there was room at the end of the tunnel for both of us at once."

"How about our tunneling out at an angle, this side of the entrance?"

"You saw the passage. Solid rock."

41

Dissatisfied, Edward went back by himself to the tunnel. They had to get out. Who was it who said there was a solution to every puzzle if you worked at it hard enough? There wasn't even a crack of light as he neared the entrance.

"No way," Ron had said. How right he was. Edward's pressure against the weight that blocked the opening was as effective as a wet noodle. His head began to buzz as if it housed a swarm of gnats.

"Did you figure a way to get us out?" Scotty demanded when he returned.

"Sure, I phoned for a bulldozer. Relax, we'll think of something."

"Big deal. You expect us to sit around here and starve to death?" Scotty swung the tin pail in one hand and clutched his hammer in the other. "I saw this TV program, see, where two fellows got stuck in a cave without any food or water and they knew it was curtains, and after they got out . . ."

"How'd they get out?" Edward cut in.

"It was really neat. One of 'em found this ring in a corner of the cave; and when he pressed the ruby, the laser beam cut a hole in the rocks and they walked out."

Scotty's fantasizing, tiresome though it might be, stirred up Edward's brain cells. "Ron, are we sure there aren't any openings in these walls? Let's examine them inch by inch."

Ron agreed, rather to satisfy him than with any hope, Edward sensed, and flicked on the flashlight which he had turned off to conserve the batteries. The three moved slowly along the walls, straining their eyes for any hint of a crevice, running their hands over the stony surface. The tapping of Scotty's hammer echoed hollowly in their ears as he went ahead, until he stubbed his toe and stumbled on the rough floor.

He groaned. "I've had it with my knee. This is the third time today I've skinned it." He had stumbled on a pile of rubble which Edward was sure hadn't been there when they entered the cave.

"If the earthquake knocked all that rock loose," he ventured, "maybe it shook up the whole wall."

Ron played the light over the area, then with a smothered exclamation held it steady just above the crumbled limestone. The wall showed a long jagged crack, like a streak of lightning, which broke open into a small triangular fissure near the floor. Edward kicked at it experimentally, and rock broke off, sending a fine powder into the air.

"Here, let me." Scotty tapped the edge of the crack with his hammer, and the rotten limestone fell away in chunks.

"Boy!" he crowed. "Was I ever sharp to bring this hammer. This thing may save our lives, you know that?" He was chipping away at the rock as he spoke. "Nobody else had the brains to bring a hammer, but I lugged it all the way up the mountain and now I know why."

He slammed his tool against the rock again, so

43

hard this time that the head flew off. "For crying out loud, what kind of a crummy hammer is this, anyway?" He threw the handle at the opposite wall and sat back on his heels.

Ron shoved the flashlight into his hands. "Hold this, Tiger. But don't stand too close to me." He picked up the head of the broken hammer and began knocking it against the fissure. Edward chopped at the opening with the blunt end of Ron's hatchet and even used his hands to pull at the limestone. Bit by bit, the rock broke off in small chunks. They stayed with it, hardly feeling the cuts and bruises on their fingers. They worked feverishly, losing all idea of time in the urgency of what they were doing. At last there was a narrow slit, and Edward strained his eyes to look through. To his consternation, he could see nothing.

The others looked in turn.

"There may be a tree trunk or a black boulder right in front of us," Ron suggested.

They redoubled their efforts, and in a dazzling piece of good fortune, a large triangular slab split off in one piece.

"That did it!" Scotty crowed.

Ron gave Edward a lighthearted swat on the rear, and he wriggled through on his hands and knees, shutting his eyes against the powdery shower raining down from contact with the edges of the fissure. When he opened them, to his confusion he was still in the dark. Where he had ex-

pected daylight, grass, and warm earth, his groping hands met only the coldness of cave rock. He
called for the flashlight, and when he flicked it on
he understood. He was not out on the mountainside but merely in an adjoining chamber of the
cave.

It appeared to be a long room with a sloping
floor—the feeble light picked up only shadows at
the far end—and he thought, I'm probably the first
human being that ever laid eyes on this place. But
the momentary thrill was swallowed up in the
chilling realization that they were no better off
than before.

Scotty and Ron crawled through the opening.

"Maybe this is where the treasure is hidden,"
said Scotty as he took in the situation. "Come on,
let's go."

Ron grabbed his arm. "Cool it. I've got something to say to both of you." His tone was deadly
serious as he briefly sketched the dangers that now
faced them. There was no alternative to going forward, but they would have to watch every step as
they advanced into unknown territory, for one
false move in the dark might plunge them down a
chute or into an abyss. If they lost their foothold on
slippery rocks, they could slide into a chasm or
drop into some bottomless lake.

Edward hoped Scotty realized what they were
all up against. His young brother evidently had
more sense than the family had given him credit

for, since he'd made it all the way up the mountain without any mishaps except for his brush with a skunk.

"We've got to use our heads to stay alive," Ron finished his lecture. "We've flunked all the rules of a good caver because we didn't expect to be caving. A real spelunker carries equipment like Prusik slings, a carbide lamp on his helmet and nylon rope. We don't have that kind of gear, but we can observe their rules."

"Such as?"

"Well, Tiger, never explore alone. There are three of us, and that's better than two. Always walk, never run. And never take a step in the dark."

"I know," Scotty said impatiently. "Is there anything to drink? I'm awful thirsty."

Ron produced the thermos bottle. "This may have to last a while," he warned as he handed it over.

7

Narrow Passages

THEY ADVANCED CAUTIOUSLY in the newly discovered cavern. Every time a passage kinked or they made their way around a clutter of rock, Edward was sure they'd see a shaft of daylight.

There had to be a way out—his mind wouldn't accept the ultimate failure. And yet people died all the time from disasters: mine cave-ins, fires, earthquakes, hurricanes, floods. Acts of God, they called them. Odd, the bad things that happened were tagged as acts of God. But God (he felt a surge of relief) wouldn't let them die.

"Low roof ahead," Ron called out. What was he thinking about their situation? Edward wasn't about to discuss it openly, but he longed to hear Ron's appraisal of their predicament. His friend hadn't shown any panic, but that didn't mean anything, for he was the type that kept cool.

They slowed their pace, and the flashlight glimmered over a tumbled pile of stairstep rocks which went sharply downhill. They descended—Scotty's pail dangling from his belt where he had fastened it with a piece of cord he'd had in his pocket—pressed through a narrow passage, and found themselves in an extraordinary place.

Ron beamed the light around an immense crescent-shaped chamber, a room for giants, the ceiling lofty, and massive columns and great boulders scattered at random. Off to one side Edward heard the drip of water and was conscious of glistening clay banks. There was a dank, earthy smell in the place, which Ron explained might mean a river or lake down in the heart of the mountain.

They started on again, and presently their feeble light picked up the mouth of a shaft in the shadows ahead of them. They drew closer and saw that it was smooth and deep, snaking down and down into the blackness.

"Hold it!" barked Ron. He picked up a loose stone and tossed it into the shaft. After what seemed an eternity they heard it rattle far below.

Scotty crowded against Edward. "Fall in there and you've had it."

They groped on, always downhill, skirted some grotesque monsters of dark stone, climbed over piles of loose rock, and finally were confronted by a choice of two passages which angled in different directions.

48

"Which one shall we take?" Edward wondered aloud.

Scotty said stubbornly, "I'm not going anyplace until I've eaten my lunch."

"Good idea," Ron said.

They sat down in the dust of centuries and drew out their sandwiches.

Scotty's aroma had faded considerably, and their spirits revived with the food, especially when Scotty shared his broken candy bars, boasting that he had enough rations left in his pockets to feed them all for a week. As they ate, they discussed plans for their next move.

Ron suggested that they begin with the right-hand corridor, but they would mark the entrance with foil from the candy bars so they could easily identify it if they had to come back and try the alternate passage. "We don't want to get lost and cover the same ground twice." Ron might not be an experienced speleologist but he used his head, thought Edward.

The corridor they chose twisted narrowly between high walls, and finally shrank to a crawlway. "Guess we'd better go through. Don't want to miss a bet," Ron decided.

He slipped off his rucksack and, pushing it before him, squirmed into the squeezeway, the others literally on his heels. "We'll take our time. If it gets too tight we'll have to back out again, and that's not easy."

They inched along until the crawlway widened, bringing them into a chamber whose spectacular beauty, even under the dim flicker of the flashlight, stopped them short. Here at last, Edward saw, were all the sights he had looked for in Pirates' Cave. The area glittered in the gloom with stalagmites and stalactites, some enormous, others as delicate as jeweled daggers. There were columns like glass pillars; stone streamers hung in graceful folds from the arched roof; a formation resembling a huge pineapple rose up from the floor; and over against one wall, the light picked up the semblance of a marble throne. The magnificent beauty of this underground room took his breath away.

"The other chamber was the Viking Hall; this is the Throne Room." Edward was trying to remember what he had read about limestone formations in caves, that water hung on the ceiling and as each drop evaporated it left a thin residue of crystal limestone. After hundreds, maybe thousands of years, this built up, or down, rather, to form stalactites. The drops that moved fast enough to fall to the floor built up, and when the two met, they formed a column.

Limestone formations could be of a great variety of bizarre shapes, which was what made caves fascinating. Sometimes water ran along an overhead crack in the cave and left a deposit all along the crack. This might grow into an apron, or curtain. You wouldn't think solid stone could look so graceful. Cave onyx, the speleologists called it.

Scotty clutched his arm. "Hey, you guys. There are seashells in the rock. How come, way up in a mountain?"

"Yup, and look at that waterfall over there. Sure looks real." Ron held the light on the formation.

In some dim lost age, limestone and flowstone had created all this beauty. There was mystery here, a feeling of silent centuries of sparkling splendor. Edward felt his mind stretching to include a far mightier Creator than he had ever envisioned.

"Funny to think of this being here for maybe millions of years" (there was awe in Ron's voice) "and no one ever seeing it before."

"And no one ever will again," piped Scotty, "if we don't get out of here to tell 'em about it."

"So we'll get out," said Edward. Actually, the chamber appeared to be a dead end. "I trust you are not going to show a pusillanimous spirit so early in our adventure."

"Show a what? What's he talking about, Ron?"

"Beats me," Ron said amiably. "But don't you run scared."

"Who's scared? I'm going to hang around long enough to find the treasure. Maybe it's stashed behind that phony waterfall. Let's look."

They prowled down the length of the fantastically beautiful cavern and came to a halt near the frozen waterfall. Behind it terraced marble slabs led to the wall.

"No treasure there," Scotty complained, with a tone of disappointment in his voice.

Edward didn't hear him, for he had become conscious of a faint green glimmer overhead. He craned his neck. Did he imagine it, or was there a stir of air from above?

He opened his mouth to speak to Ron when something he'd read came back to him. Green stains in caves, the book had said, are caused by algae, tiny primitive organisms which are prolific and can survive for long periods without moisture. Such microscopic plants contain a cell of green pigment. Was the green which the flashlight had momentarily picked up merely algae?

Then he felt it on his face again; he was sure it was a waft of air. When he called it to the others' attention, Scotty immediately clamored, "Let's climb up and see."

Ron swept the flashlight over the area. "It would be simple with spelunking gear. Maybe even without it," he amended thoughtfully. "Look at all the toeholds."

It might not be impossible for Ron, with his long legs and steel-coil muscles. Edward estimated the height of the wall at 35 or 40 feet. Still, he'd have to do it in the dark, and even with all those toeholds the least misstep would mean disaster. Let fingers or feet slip, and his skull would crack on the stone floor like a ripe pumpkin. Did that greenish glimmer justify the risk?

Ron answered Edward's unspoken question. "It's worth a try, but first I'd like to go back to that other passageway and find out where it goes.... No use dragging you two along," he added.

"You said yourself it isn't safe to explore alone," Edward objected.

Ron, standing close to him, said in his ear, "Safer than taking Tiger. He worries me some."

Scotty overheard him.

"I'm not staying here alone!"

"No question of that," Edward said absently. Was it a good idea to remain behind while Ron made a quick survey of the other passage? True, he would make better time without Scotty to worry about; besides, sitting here on the floor for an hour or so, even in the dark, sounded good. He didn't know when he'd felt so beat. The other corridor might lead to a dead end, and they'd have made their trip for nothing and would have to come all the way back here anyway.

But what if Ron ran into problems all by himself? Edward spoke in an unexpectedly firm voice. "We'll all go. We're sticking together, Ron."

8

Ancient Sights

THE RETURN TO VIKING HALL was tiresome, and Edward was glad when they found the identifying scraps of foil and turned into the left-hand corridor.

The passage widened as they proceeded, but they couldn't hurry even so, for it twisted like a corkscrew, making it impossible to see more than a few feet ahead. At last it broadened considerably and it became apparent that they had entered another huge chamber.

They clambered over a slope of rubble and went on, pressing close to the clammy wall. When the flashlight began to flicker alarmingly, they came to an abrupt halt and Ron turned it off to rest the batteries. That's all we need, Edward thought, to have the flashlight conk out. Ron would have extra batteries, though, foresighted as he was.

After a moment the light beamed steadily again and Ron swept it over the long stretch of scratched gray stone wall. As he did so, Edward gave a startled exclamation. Under the sweep of the light a shape had leaped out, the outline of an animal. "Wait, Ron, give us a light over here."

They all stood staring as the wall that had looked like nothing but a mass of jagged furrows became a picture gallery when the light caught it just right. Here was outlined a leaping deer, primitive, realistic; there, a bear looking up with lowered head. Above the bear Edward made out an eagle with spread wings, and near it a small animal which might have been a rabbit.

"People used to live here—about a billion years ago, I bet." Scotty's voice was subdued.

"Troglodytes. We had Cro-Magnon man last semester. They were fabulous artists." Edward couldn't repress his rising excitement. "You know, this could be the treasure of Squaw Mountain. When we get home and report these pictures, watch things hum."

"Rats! This isn't half as good as a chest of diamonds and emeralds and stuff."

Ron snapped off the flashlight. "Don't overlook one other little fact."

"What's that?"

"If human beings lived here in the cave, there must be an entrance we haven't discovered."

"Far out!" breathed Scotty.

A wave of relief swept over Edward. God was looking after them as he'd always known, deep down, He would. Now he could give himself up to the enjoyment of their discovery. The things they'd have to recount when they got back to Cleveland! The cave lost its horror and became a pleasantly exciting area.

They came to the brink of a deep crevasse where, far below, he saw the gleam of moving waters. They skirted it calmly, crawled along a narrow ledge, and climbed over a sharp blade of rock. It was as they detoured around some high, tumbled slabs that Edward caught, at eye level, a prick of light. It was the merest flash, and he told himself sternly that it was not necessarily significant, but he couldn't repress the leap of his heart. Apparently the others hadn't yet seen it, and he remained silent as they walked toward it. He wasn't prepared for the jolt he felt when they drew closer and the light proved to be merely the sparkle from an area of quartz. It glittered like diamonds, sending out spears of light. A cave mirage, you could call it.

It wasn't only the immediate disappointment that hit him. The thought lodged like a stone in his mind that no doubt the light in the Throne Room was a similar "mirage."

They moved on, but a listlessness was creeping over him. Nothing mattered, nothing would ever change. They would walk endlessly, never reaching their goal, frustrated, trapped, starving, thirst-ridden, until they fell exhausted and dying on the cold stones.

He shook himself. Caves impaired an individual's judgment after a certain period of time, he'd read. He—all of them—would have to be on their guard to fight off depression and the sense of uselessness.

He plodded on behind the unusually silent Scotty. He had lost all sense of time. Had they been on their way an hour or all afternoon?

Ron halted at last, and Edward saw that their way was blocked by a huge rockslide. Ron said, almost indifferently, that it might have been the work of the earthquake earlier that day. Whatever had caused it, they couldn't go any farther.

Drearily they turned to retrace their steps when Ron stopped short. A sweep of the flashlight had revealed a niche in the wall to the left of the slide.

"Hold the light, Ed." He climbed over the rockslide almost on hands and knees toward the recess. Before he reached it, however, he called back, "It's only an alcove."

He had turned and begun picking his way back to them when, without warning, the loose rock slid and he went careening to the base of the slide. He tried to rise, and sank back with a smothered exclamation.

Edward was alarmed. "What's the matter?"

"Of all the rotten luck." He could not put his

weight on his foot. When he unlaced his boot and stripped off his sock, the flashlight showed a purpling ankle.

"It's not too bad." Ron massaged it with both hands. "Give me a few minutes to rest it—I'll keep it hoisted on this rock to let the swelling go down—and I'll be ready to walk with a little help."

Edward sat down beside him. "Is it pretty painful?"

"It's OK. What time is it, anyway?" He held his wristwatch under the light. As he did so, the beam flickered and went out. He clicked the switch several times, but it would not come on again.

In the stunned silence that followed, he groaned, "Oh no! And me with no extra batteries."

· "No extra—?" stammered Edward.

"Call me stupid. Call me anything you please," Ron mumbled.

"We've got matches," Edward offered weakly after a moment. But he knew right away they'd have to be saved for dire emergencies.

Scotty spoke finally. "I s'pose Mom's eating dinner now and wondering where I am. I told her I was going to Tim Gesswein's. She thinks I'm drowned."

"Don't you believe it. She's checked with the Gessweins, and guessed the truth. She thinks we're all camping out on the mountain."

"And if we don't show up tomorrow—"

"They'll send out a search party for us," Ron said quickly.

Scotty, relieved, dropped the subject. "I'm hungry. Let's eat. You want some of my lunch?"

He began digging in his pockets and then suddenly made the explosive "Zing!" which always accompanied his gesture of aiming a pistol at his head and pulling the trigger. "Wrap me up and mail me to the zoo! You know what? Hey, you guys, you know what? Wait till you see this!"

9

A Test of Courage

IT WOULD BE SCOTTY, Edward thought resignedly, who shed light on their dark situation when he and Ron were at their wits' end. When Scotty brought out the candles he'd carried in his pockets, Ron's foot had crashed off the rock. "You've got to be kidding."

Although seated, Scotty gave the impression of prancing. "Hee, hee! Nobody thought of candles but me. I'm the only one who brought candles."

Edward sighed. His brother *would* be insufferable now.

While they munched Scotty's brownies, they discussed their next move. Ron felt it was important to return to the Throne Room and investigate the possible opening as quickly as they could.

Edward agreed. "You behold in me the human fly. I shall speed up that wall in nothing flat."

"Great. Let's go." Ron stood to test his ankle. "I can make it if I rest along the way."

They lit a candle, Edward drew Ron's arm across his shoulder, and the trio set out on their return journey. It was slow work. They took care to follow the precise trail they had blazed earlier, and in the dim flare of the candle they reached the quartz slope, where Ron rested.

Then, keeping close to the wall, they went on again, through the "Art Gallery" and along the corkscrew passage. Ron limped doggedly along, speaking through clenched teeth only to answer a question or make a suggestion.

Limp forward, rest, limp on again. It was an agonizing journey that seemed to have no end, but at last they reached the squeezeway. Would Ron be able to handle it? Somehow he crawled through, and then they were in the Throne Room. It was nine o'clock.

They were exhausted. Nothing more could be done until morning, so Scotty removed the contents of his pockets, laying them out on the stones beside his tin pail, and stretched out. Almost at once he was dead to the world. Edward and Ron talked then, in murmurs.

"I'm not a complete novice, Ron. I climbed a wall last summer. Not as steep as this one, but the same principle was involved."

"I'm surprised your mother didn't squawk."

He grinned in the dark. "You sometimes have to

operate on the theory that what a person doesn't know won't hurt her."

"I guess mothers would have heart attacks a dozen times a day if they knew what their kids were into. But I can't forget," Ron groaned, "that I was the one who told your mother this hike was as safe as a church."

"You don't pretend to take credit for the earthquake, do you? That *is* presumption."

"Ha! If you do go up the wall, Ed, and if there is an opening, and if you get out of the cave, you'll still have to find the trail, get down to Musket Beach, and guide a party back here. It's a big order."

"I can do it." There was a cold lump in his stomach.

"Light the candle again, will you? Here's the matchbox." Ron tore off a scrap of paper from his lunch bag, and by candlelight sketched a crude map, in line with his estimate of their position and where Tomahawk Trail lay in relation to it.

"I figure we're about here." He penciled an X on the paper. "I tried to keep track of distance and direction as we came through the cave. If you can get out of the opening and you keep going in a westerly direction from the cave, you ought to come out on the trail below the fallen tree, the way I figure it. You'll have the compass."

It looked so simple, on paper.

They lay down on the cold floor, close together

for warmth, and Edward finally heard Ron's deep breathing. He himself turned restlessly on the hard surface, searching for a spot that wouldn't jab his ribs. It wasn't the physical discomfort that was keeping him awake, however.

He thought of his mother. She had probably notified his father by this time, and both of them would be anxious. There was one thing Mom would be doing, though, and that was praying. She prayed about everything, like even putting a cake in the oven. The POWs had prayed, too, and the astronauts. He shook off a sense of shame at running to God when he was in trouble, when he had ignored Him so much of the time. He knew enough about Him to know He never turned away anybody who meant business. And he did for sure. Their lives might depend on his climbing that wall, and he didn't have what it would take. "I'll do my best, but it won't be good enough. You'll have to take over," he begged of that Presence that he was becoming increasingly aware of. Calmed, he fell asleep.

It was seven o'clock by Ron's wristwatch when Edward started up the wall the next morning. His peace of mind still held. He had shed his bulky jacket, jammed the compass, the matches and the map into his jeans pocket. Ron and Scotty remained behind with their lighted candles while Ron pointed out the best route of ascent. As Edward craned his neck toward the ceiling, he observed something he hadn't noticed before; there seemed to be a ledge in the shadows near the top of the wall.

"Good." Ron leaned against the wall on one foot. "If you can pull yourself up onto that shelf, you can get your bearings from there. If you have to come down again it'll give you a breather first."

Edward's stomach lurched. Come down?

"Don't take all day getting back up here with ropes and stuff, Edward," Scotty ordered. "We've got nothing to do all day but sit here, remember. And the thermos is empty."

"My heart bleeds for you. All set, Ron."

Those little candles weren't much help. He'd have to go more by memory than sight. Luckily he had taken a long look at the wall. He put his toe into a wide niche and reached for a handhold. He'd never make it to the top; he wasn't in Ron's league. He'd get sick and dizzy and everything would go black.

He drew himself up and felt for the next toehold, his face pressed against the cold stone. He hated heights, no getting around it. It had been just a lucky fluke that he'd ever made it up that church wall. If he'd chickened out before he got to the top, someone would have rescued him, but there was no one here to help—except God! He'd never had to depend on Him for his very life before, not consciously anyway, but he sure was depending on Him now.

The light moved up and he moved with it. Getting a foothold wasn't so bad, but gripping those little hunks of protruding rock with damp, slippery fingers was murder. Another step, and his seeking fingers found another jagged projection and he drew himself up.

The thing was not to look down, not even to think, but just find that toehold, get hold of an edge of rock to latch onto, and keep going. Shuddering, spread-eagled against the cold wall, he crept upward. He moved his left foot, couldn't find a place for the right one, and hung precariously. He was tiring—his legs and arms ached and he was panting. Then he saw a half-inch niche and pulled himself up.

"Attaboy!" he heard Ron mutter a world away as he moved, and moved again.

Cold sweat was rolling into his eyes when the ledge appeared above his head. He clung, despairing. The only way he could get a knee up on it was to let go with one hand and throw an arm across the ledge. It was a risk he'd have to take. He acted with the speed of light and got one knee over the edge somehow. Then, his breath rattling in his throat, he hauled himself up and sank onto the narrow ledge. He felt like a soppy wad of tissue.

"What d'ya see?" Ron's voice from below sounded hoarse.

He drew himself up to a kneeling position. Wow! His voice strained the first time, then he steadied it. "It's a big opening. I can get out easily."

"No kidding? How much of a drop?"

"Nothing to it. There's a fallen tree just outside. It's the branches—the leaves—that give the green light down there."

"Green light is right," chortled Scotty. "Go on out. I'm coming up too."

"Nothing doing, Scotty," Edward barked. "Lose your footing and your skull would crack on the stones like a rotten egg."

"Thanks a lot." He could hear his brother gagging exaggeratedly. "You just talked me out of it."

He swung out and dropped to the ground. He blinked in the golden light and when he tried to stand, his knees buckled. An instant later his protesting stomach had its way. He was thankful the others weren't there to see him.

Edward lay quietly for a few minutes, but gradually the freshness of the air and the beauty of the July morning revived him. He stood up. So this was how a worm felt when he came up from the earth for air.

An early sun rimmed the distant peaks with gold, and the grass sparkled with dew. A narrow, grassy plateau stretched northward for perhaps 300 yards. It was fringed with evergreens along its east border, where the sun turned the sky to fire. To the west, where his route lay, the plateau rose to a ridge.

He turned and gazed curiously at the cave open-

67

ing. You'd never guess what lay within that little hillock, where spikes of coarse grass stuck up between the scattered stones, and a stiff-legged robin hopped here and there.

Above the treetops to his rear he saw some high bluffs. He wasn't concerned with what lay to the south, however, and turned toward the ridge. This was no time to stand around gaping at the scenery. He had a mission to accomplish.

Compass in hand, he struck off across the plateau. Ron had figured it might take him an hour or more to intersect Tomahawk Trail, but he could really roll from then on, be home by noon, and back up here with men and ropes by evening. They might all have to camp out on the mountain tonight, but Scotty would think that was great.

He hadn't felt so lighthearted since he was a little kid. He hoped he wouldn't encounter any deep gorges or a lot of thickets or outcroppings of rock that would slow him, but he could handle it, whatever came up.

He squinted under the sun's brilliance. It was hard to believe that the blue sky, with its gobs of whipped-cream clouds, had just yesterday been swollen and angry, spitting yellow-green light and booming like a battlefield.

He gained the ridge, looked over and stood frozen. He had expected shallow descents, grassy slopes, or little rocky gullies to lead him back to Tomahawk Trail, but he was on the edge of a prec-

ipice. The ridge dropped off sheer beneath him.
The emptiness below gave him a dizzy sensation as
if he were hurtling through the air, and he drew
back.

There would be a break in the plunging cliff
farther along the promontory. All he needed was a
spur of rock, a little sloping terrace, anything that
would drop him down from the plateau, spanning
the gap to the canyon floor. He turned and hiked
along the lip of the cliff, but saw only the massed
tops of the evergreens as he hurried along. At the
rounded tip of the plateau, pinnacles of rock stuck
up breast high to form a rampart. He leaned his
forearms on this wall and looked over. Nothing!

More slowly now, he continued along the east
side of the stony little wasteland until he came to a
fringe of woods opposite the cave opening. In all
that distance there had not been a single means of
descent. Heartbreak Ridge, he said to himself. And
it was hopeless, of course, to the south, where the
bluffs sprang upward.

His exploration had revealed nothing that even
a mountain goat would opt for. It's like being on a
peninsula, he thought confusedly, suspended in
space. He pictured the stony shelf of land sticking
out from the side of the mountain, closed in by high
cliffs behind and dropping off in a sheer precipice
all around. As the image sharpened in his mind,
the truth hit like a staggering blow. He was on the
Squaw's Nose.

10

Squaw's Nose

EDWARD COLLAPSED ON A FLAT ROCK and shook his head to clear it. He was trapped on the Squaw's Nose and his two companions were still imprisoned in the cave. Now what did he do?

But whoa! Was he sure of his facts? Maybe his imagination was working overtime. No, it all checked out. Ron had said the Nose was inaccessible from either below or above, and this plateau was just that. True, he still had to examine at close range the bluffs which walled in this little neck of land, but from here they looked as sheer and unbroken as gray glass. Would closer observation prove them to be scalable at some point?

And what if they were? He wouldn't be up to a tough climb up a cliff of that height. Still, if there should prove to be a lot of broken rock and crevices, he knew he'd take a chance before he'd let his brother and Ron die inside the cave.

He had wasted enough time sitting here, and he started toward the bluffs. Before he got very far, however, he saw that it would be smart to clue Ron in on his findings, dismaying though they might be. Two heads were better than one, as long as they weren't on the same neck. His feet dragged, though, as he neared the cave.

A limb of the fallen tree outside the opening jabbed him as he clambered onto the trunk. He stopped dead and gave the tree a considering look. Was it a kooky idea? Could he lift it? Would it work? He jumped off and leaned down to test its weight, his heart beating fast. Not too bad, but he needed to get it closer. He tugged and it moved, its branches dragging in the dirt. Grunting, he pushed and pulled until he had it where he wanted it. His mouth had become dry from all of the excitement.

"Come on, adrenaline," he implored as he strained to lift the dead weight toward the opening. He'd never make it. Ron could probably pick this thing up with one hand, but he, Edward, didn't have what it takes.

He heaved with all his strength and the log lifted. It was off the ground and his shoulder muscles strained as he thrust it slowly upward and into the opening.

"Stand clear!" he shouted to the two below.

He stood for a minute to get his breath, ignoring the loud questions which peppered him from be-

low. So far, so good, but he'd never be able to shove
it in the rest of the way.

With an unvoiced prayer he tackled it again,
fighting the log foot by foot until a shout from
below told him he'd won.

Scotty came up first, scooting up the trunk with
his tin pail clanking at his waist. He wore Edward's red windbreaker on top of his own faded
blue one. He jumped to the ground, then turned
and hauled up Ron's boots on the cord tied to his
wrist.

Then Ron squirmed his way up, grasping the
branches for leverage, and emerged to stand like a
stork in the sunlight outside the cave.

Edward's relief momentarily crowded out his
apprehension. He kicked at the litter of branches
underfoot until he uncovered a stout limb that
would do for a walking stick, and handed it to Ron.
I won't tell him, he thought. Let him discover the
truth for himself. People are apt to blame you for
the bad tidings you bring them.

Ron's diagnosis, as Edward led the way on a tour
of inspection, was not long in coming. He stood at
the ramparts, leaning on his stick. "Afraid I've got
bad news." He looked at Scotty doubtfully.

Scotty wasn't listening. "You know something?
We're on the Squaw's Nose, that's where."

Edward felt humiliated to see how much faster
they'd caught on than he had. "Just think, no
human being has ever set foot on this turf before."

73

"It figures!" snorted Scotty. His jacket gaped open, there was a three-cornered tear in the knee of his dusty jeans, and his round face, topped with his dirty cap, was scratched and streaked with berry juice and dirt. "We'd naturally land in some dumb place where nobody else ever wanted to be caught dead. How long are we going to be stuck up here, for crying out loud?"

"At a venture, I'd say until our patient is recovered."

Scotty groaned.

"Come, come, my boy." Edward wagged his head. "Why this note of dissatisfaction? Aren't you the one who has been preaching the joys of camping?"

Scotty caught just one word. "Camping?" He danced on his toes and jabbed with his fists at an imaginary foe. "We're camping out! We're camping out! We'll build a big fire and tell ghost stories and sleep under the stars. Wait till Tim hears about this."

Ron looked at Edward with a skeptical expression. "You didn't explore to the south? You wouldn't have had time."

"No, but look how high those bluffs are."

But Ron wanted to have a look at close range. His ankle was killing him, but he hobbled over the uneven ground toward the bluffs, and Edward followed, filled with admiration for the other boy's thoroughness. That was what made Ron so great in the outdoors: never taking anything for granted. On the mountains or in the woods your life might depend on such thoroughness.

Their hike led them up a gentle slope behind the cave site. As they came to the top of the rise they stopped in their tracks. At their feet lay a sunny little meadow folded between the woods on the east and the ridge on the west. The colorful little bowl was blanketed with lush green grass and thousands of miniature bright-colored flowers. The hum of mountain bees throbbed in the fragrant air like an organ note, and a cloud of white butterflies drifted over a nearby clump of wild honeysuckle.

Then above the drone of the bees they heard it—a sound that jackknifed Scotty into action. He crashed down the slope, trampling the tiny flowers underfoot as he dashed toward a thin line of willows. At his loud yell Edward broke into a jog, and Ron began working his way painfully down the hillside after them.

The stream that tumbled out of the bluffs was a thread of silver meandering across the meadow. The boys flung themselves down on its bank and buried their faces in the water, so icy it made them gasp. They drank as if they were camels and had two stomachs to fill; then they tore off their jackets and shirts and plunged their arms and heads into the water.

Ron sat back finally and swiped at his face with a

wet hand. "Somebody up there is watching out for us, right?"

Edward was abashed that the acknowledgment had come from Ron, who had no particular religious convictions so far as he had been able to discover. "I knew that when I made it up the wall," he said in an effort to atone for his tardy testimony.

Ron turned to stare at him. "That 30-foot climb?"

Edward felt himself reddening. He had only been trying to give honor to whom it was due. And I'd like to put a tape measure on that wall, he thought.

Scotty had turned over on his back and lay blissfully gazing at the cloud formations, while Ron chewed on a grass stem and studied the bluffs across the stream.

"There's bound to be some kind of a break in those cliffs where a fellow could climb up. We can take a good look later; but since we have water, there's no hurry." Ron tossed away his chewed stem and selected another.

Scotty turned a handspring. "What'll we do, eat roots and berries like they do in stories when they're cast on a desert island?"

"You've hit it, Tiger, right on the Nose." Ron grinned.

Scotty's face lengthened. "I wasn't serious, for crying out loud. I don't go for carrots and spinach even when Mom dopes 'em up with butter and orange rind and stuff."

"Wait till your stomach walls begin to grind," Edward prophesied. "You'll even be glad to eat snails."

Scotty gagged. "Not while I've got hot dogs in my pocket."

"Got what?"

Scotty pulled a plastic package, somewhat the worse for wear, out of one pocket. "Mom is probably wondering what happened to 'em. She wasn't looking when I took 'em."

"That makes four," Edward said resignedly. "The hammer, the candles, the cord, and now this. I can't bear it."

"Yeah, you might have died up here without me," Scotty crowed. "If it hadn't been for me, you'd really be messed up. I'm the one . . ."

Edward sailed a grass clod at the obnoxious boy, and Ron suggested that everyone quit clowning so they could take inventory of their possessions and see where they stood.

Scotty emptied his pockets of two squashed peanut butter and jelly sandwiches, a good-sized chunk of cheese, four brownies, some raisins and a hard-boiled egg, along with his slingshot, a knife with a broken blade, a wad of cord, and a starfish. The others added a waterproof box of matches, two empty thermos bottles, a hatchet, a scout knife, a small first-aid kit, the compass, an empty plastic sack, and Edward's allergy pills.

"Forgot all about 'em," Edward said, eyeing the

77

bottle sheepishly. "Matter of fact, I haven't sneezed since we went into the cave."

"I've heard that cave atmosphere cures some allergies," Ron said.

They divided the sandwiches and cheese among them, stowed everything else in the rucksack for future use, and while they ate they discussed what their first move should be.

"We should pick a campsite," Ron said. "We'll be here a few days, remember." He pulled up the leg of his levis to let them see his swollen ankle.

They selected a level place between the stream and the woods, near a jumble of rock where they would build their fire. At Ron's direction, Edward and Scotty placed stones in a circle to contain their fire, positioning them near the biggest boulder to reflect the heat. Then they brought firewood from the woods while Ron, his back against a rock, whittled at a chip. The firewood gathered, he sent them to the woods again, this time to cut fir boughs for their beds. "They shouldn't be any thicker than a pencil," he cautioned, "and the more you use the softer your mattress will be. We'll need a lot of them for three beds."

The slender fir branches were easier to hack off with the knife and hatchet than they expected, and the two boys brought back armful after armful. Can't worry about saving the wilderness, Edward decided.

When they had enough, Ron showed them how

to press the coarse, stalky end of a branch down toward the ground and overlap it with another one. They repeated this over and over until they had five or six layers of branches, a tedious task, but one for which they felt well repaid when they tried out their fragrant mattresses.

Edward flopped down on his own. His legs and arms ached and he was ravenously hungry, but there was still work to be done. He watched with interest as Ron heaped brittle twigs and dry needles inside the circle of stones, and then produced the chip which he had whittled into shavings, so that it looked like a comb. He applied a match to this "fire stick" and held it to the twigs. They blazed up, and he carefully added more cones and slender dead sticks. In a moment the fire was crackling.

As the shadows lengthened, they crouched about their fire, sniffing the odors of the hot dogs roasting on sticks while the juice dripped and sizzled on the burning logs.

Scotty smacked his lips over the last blackened bite. "Now for the blueberry pie with ice cream, or a big hunk of chocolate cake." He fell backward over his log as he saw Edward coming for him with bared teeth and fingers curved like talons.

A little breeze stirred the tops of the alders, and an owl hooted softly from the woods. Scotty was out the instant he hit the sack, arms flung like a scarecrow, legs sprawled.

Their situation was precarious, but as Edward lay looking up at the brilliant stars pricking the darkening sky, they seemed to be saying, "The hand that guides us in our courses will hold you fast."

11

Fish and Wild Roots

THE SUN WAS WARM on Edward's eyelids. He blinked and opened his eyes on a meadow glittering like a jeweler's window. The call of a bird from the woods was like the silvery note of a flute.

The smoke drifting up from the campfire sent messages to his stomach of bacon sizzling in the pan along with four or five yellow-eyed eggs, of a stack of hotcakes with the syrup dripping down the sides, or maybe waffles with the butter melting into the little squares and the blueberry syrup flowing over them. Those little pork sausages were good, too, along with thick golden brown toast, crisp on the outside but soft inside, the raspberry jam spread an inch thick over it.

He was wide awake now. His stomach felt like a collapsed balloon, and he knew there were only a few brownies and a handful of raisins left. How long could they live on berries? People did exist a long time without food; it was water that was the great necessity, and the gurgle of the stream not far away was immensely cheering.

The fire had burned low and he moved to replenish it. He glanced over at Ron as the flame blazed up. The other boy was sleeping heavily. His cheekbones were prominent in his brown face, and his ankle looked swollen even under his heavy sock. He had been on his feet too much yesterday, but from now on he could take it easy.

Scotty was wound up like a snail, one lock of hair standing straight up on his head.

Edward picked his way through the dewy grass to the stream, drawing the crisp air deep into his lungs and noting the crystal drops caught in the gauzy spider webs which draped the vines.

Brrr! The water was icy. As he shook the drops out of his eyes, a brown form darted downstream. He thought he knew where the big fish was headed, for he had noticed yesterday that the stream widened farther down to a placid pool.

He pushed through the undergrowth on the bank until he found it, just below a tinkling little waterfall, and his heart beat faster as he observed half a dozen big fish sliding in and out among the stones. Those fellows should be easy to catch, since they knew nothing of man and his wicked ways. You could almost catch them with your bare hands. Hey, how about that?

He stretched out on the bank and had hardly settled himself when an immense shape slid out from under a rock, a veritable submarine of a fish. Edward pounced before he thought. The giant was way ahead of him, flirting his tail in ridicule, but to Edward's surprise he found himself gripping a smaller fish which had been caught in the moss. Aha, he had him. He brought him out on the bank, where he flopped and struggled. Poor fish! Why did something always have to die in order that something else might live? But he couldn't be sorry, for that trout would help to make them a yummy breakfast.

He'd probably scared the giant off for a while, but a 12-incher wasn't bad. He put his hands very quietly into the water this time, and lifted out another.

He caught two more before the fish grew wary of his octopus hands. He trotted back to camp with his catch strung on a tough vine, vowing he'd have a try for Grandpappy fish later.

Ron was tossing the last wood on the fire when he arrived, and Scotty turned over, yawning, then bounded upright.

"Broth-er! Breakfast! What did you do, Ed? Pick 'em out of the water with your bare hands? You're kidding. They sure must be dumb."

"What'll we do without a frying pan, Ron? Eat 'em raw?"

"Not on your life. We'll need some flat rocks to

heat in the fire, then we'll bake these fellows on the rocks over hot coals."

"You wouldn't believe the one that slid right through my digits," Edward mourned. "He must have been 20 inches or more."

"Yeah! Yeah! First time he ever caught a fish and all he can talk about is the one that got away," Scotty jeered. "Hey, Ron, I'll get the rocks out of the creek. I saw a lot of 'em yesterday."

"Get dry ones. Rocks that have been in the water explode in the fire."

"How's the ankle?" Edward asked before he went to the woods for more firewood.

"Better. Still swollen, but give me a couple of more days and I'll be OK." Ron reached for the stout stick he had begun to fashion into a crutch.

While the rocks were heating, Edward and Scotty watched Ron slit the fish lengthwise, cut the tendons that fastened the gills to the head, and then in one movement pull out both gills and intestines. He laid the big beauties on the hot rocks. "They taste good spitted on twigs, too," he observed, "Indian fashion. We'll try 'em that way next time."

Drooling, they watched their breakfast baking over the coals. Presently Ron edged the fish out of the fire, and they tore into them like starving wolves.

"The finest repast I have ever had the pleasure of masticating," Edward declared when only a few bones remained. "We're not apt to run out of fish either. The pool is lousy with them, and I do not use the word in the pejorative sense."

Scotty wiped his mouth with the back of his hand. "Whatever that means. They were good, but I'm still hungry. Well, I'll see you guys later. I've got things to do." He stooped for his cap.

"Come back here!" Edward yelled, but Scotty was already jogging across the meadow.

The rat. Did he think he was a guest at a dude ranch? There was firewood to gather, water to carry, berries to pick and fish to catch if they were to exist for the next day or two.

Seething, he hurried through the chores and left Ron whittling at his crutches as he struck off toward Heartbreak Ridge with the pail in his hand. He was itching to cross the stream and explore the bluffs, for he could hardly wait to see what their chances were over there, but it would have to wait.

The blackberries grew thick in the stony soil of the ridge. As they thunked into the pail his eyes were busy. The precipice hadn't grown any less formidable since yesterday. If they only had ropes and belays—but there was no use getting "iffy." They didn't have a thing in the world to get them out of this dilemma, nothing but their minds and their hands and feet, and *they* would be useless if the odds were too great.

He thought of his parents. What would they do if their boys never came home? Would his mother fall apart completely? What was she doing now? Praying, that was for sure. And he ought to be praying as he'd never prayed before because even Ron, competent as he was, would need more than human strength and skill to climb to the top of the bluff.

His pail was soon full and he resolved to drop it off at camp and go on to the bluffs. He couldn't stand the suspense any longer. But at camp Ron had a job for him.

"Dig up all the tubers you can. I can pick out the edible ones. Camass bulbs are great—that's wild hyacinth—and I think the blue flowers on the slope may be camass."

Edward started off, the emptied rucksack dangling from one hand and the knife from the other. It was almost noon and he'd spent the whole morning on the bare essentials of existence. No wonder some peoples of the earth never developed a high culture, having to grub all day for barely enough to eat. Who had time to paint great pictures or write soul-stirring poetry when he was digging roots all day? Still, the cave dwellers had drawn all those pictures of the life around them, so there was some creative spark in man that demanded expression, no matter how hard his life was. This was one of the things, he guessed, that set him apart from the animals, who were content merely to eat, sleep and bear their young.

He had a fair quantity of roots in the rucksack

before he saw the glimmer of blue on the slope above him. Ron's wild hyacinth. The root looked like a tulip bulb, and he got busy. Where had Ron learned so much about survival in the wilderness? He was already a long way on the road to his chosen career.

Ron grinned widely when he saw the hyacinth bulbs. "That's camass, no mistake. Is there a lot more? Great. The Indians used it like we do potatoes, boiled or baked 'em. We'll boil some in our pail because we're in a hurry, but later on I'll show you how to roast them in a pit."

Ron had thrust forked sticks into each end of the fireplace and hung the water-filled pail on a green stub over the hot coals. He had poured the blackberries into the plastic sack he had saved. While the camass simmered over the fire, he examined the remainder of the rucksack's contents.

"Squaw root—'wild carrots' to you, wild rhubarb, and you've got some Indian lettuce, and this is goosefoot."

"Looks like spinach."

"It's wild spinach. We can even eat burdock and milkweed if we get hard up. They're bitter, but if you boil them and pour off the water and cook them again in fresh water, they're edible. You've done all right by us, old buddy."

Edward felt as if he'd been decorated with the Purple Heart.

87

Digging the pit for an underground oven was the most laborious task of the day. It was slow work without a shovel, although the paddles Ron had fashioned worked fairly well. When the pit was deep enough he showed Edward how to line the bottom and sides with stones, and a fire was built over them.

"When the rocks are hot and the fire dies down to embers, we'll lay layers of green leaves over them and put our roots on top, then more leaves, and the dirt on top of them, and the bulbs can cook all night. If we had a little meat to put in with them, we'd have a banquet."

"You're causing my salivary glands to run like a river."

Edward was surprised, when he returned from the woods with an armful of branches for the oven, that Scotty hadn't come back. He glanced at his watch, which he faithfully wound each day. "Four o'clock. Where is that little bum?"

Ron pursed his lips. "Probably building a dam in the creek."

Edward cupped his hands around his mouth and shouted repeatedly, but there was only a mocking echo from the bluffs. You'd have thought hunger would have driven Scotty back to camp long before this. He'd have to go after him.

He wasn't at the waterfall or the fishing hole. Farther down he came across another oddly shaped pool, sort of like a bathtub. From here on the stream narrowed and eventually got lost in the marshy land which bordered the east side of the Nose.

He turned and hiked up to the woods, shouting for his brother as he went, but there was no trace of him. Was he goofing around at the Ramparts? Why had he turned the kid loose? He knew how accident-prone he was. What if he'd taken it into his head to try to climb down from Heartbreak Ridge?

He raced across the meadow and up the slope to the Ramparts, from where he could look both east and west, but he realized afresh when he stood there that no one, not even Scotty, would be rash enough to attempt a descent from there.

He was running out of places to look.

He checked with Ron as he passed camp again and went on toward the swamp. The little dope might possibly have waded in there and got stuck. A sudden thought struck him. Would there be quicksand in the marsh? He broke into a run.

12

Scotty's Ordeal

THE DAY HAD STARTED with a bang. Scotty set off across the sunny meadow, slapping his slingshot against his thigh and whistling "Jingle Bells." He grinned as he visualized Edward's and Ron's faces when he walked into camp with wild game slung over his shoulder.

"Bring back a squirrel and I'll teach you how to skin it!" Ron had shouted after him. Scotty had caught his sly wink.

He needed practice with his slingshot and didn't have any time to waste carrying wood and picking berries. But of course Edward never gave him any credit.

He wasn't too skilled with his weapon, he had to admit, when he'd missed his target a dozen times. This would take more practice than he'd planned on.

He plowed along through the thin strip of woods,

shooting at burls and rocks along the way, and headed toward the creek. On the way he stopped to admire an oak tree. He couldn't resist a tall tree any more than a mouse could resist the cheese in a trap, and he swarmed up the gnarled trunk. It was a neat tree. He passed the lower outspread branches and went on higher.

In a crotch above him he saw a nest, a whopper of a nest. Too bad it was too late in the season for bird's eggs. As his head rose almost to the level of the nest, he heard a whir of wings and looked up. Diving straight at him—he could see the staring yellow eyes—was a hawk prepared to strike. Instinctively Scotty threw one arm over his eyes and slid down at lightning speed, one hand grasping at whatever lent itself to brake his plunge.

Wham! A heavy bough arrested his fall. He grabbed at it with scraped and bleeding hands while the hawk soared off, screaming in triumph. It had happened so fast that only now when it was over did he feel scared.

"Huh! You can have your old tree." Shakily, he climbed on down, and from the ground watched the hawk, now a dark speck, wheeling in the sky.

He had seen a clump of berry bushes near the stream while high in the oak, and he made for them now. They proved to be blueberries, and he stuffed himself and filled his cap, forgetting his sore palms in the process. He'd take them back for lunch as a peace offering.

Near the berry patch he noticed some bees hovering near a hollow stump, and he hurried over to investigate. So that's what bees did in their spare time. The honeycomb in the stump looked good enough to eat.

He was moving in when an angry hum alerted him, and he felt a sharp tack being driven into one cheek. He saw them coming then, a whole swarm, and he pelted toward the stream with all the speed he could summon, dived into a pool that looked like a bathtub, and submerged himself.

He snickered. That was the best time he'd ever made toward a bathtub. He got out on the far side of the stream, muttering to himself, stripped, and hung his clothes on the bushes to dry. His cheek felt sore and as he pressed a forefinger against it something popped out. The stinger! He'd accidentally pushed on just the right spot. Like Mom always said, he was accident-prone. Just for good measure, though, he plastered his cheek with mud. He'd heard that was good for bee stings.

He pranced around in his birthday suit, drawing a bead on a caveman who came lunging at him, dropping a grizzly in his tracks, and standing on a stump to recite "Casey at the Bat," with appropriate gestures.

Then his conscience began to bother him. He ought to be figuring out ways to climb the bluff. Ron was taking his time about it.

His race across the rocky strip between the bank

and the bluffs was broken abruptly as he fell head-long, jarring every bone in his body in his plunge downward. He lay in a huddle at the bottom of a hole, tasting blood from his cut lip. His head hurt so much he couldn't think. Where was he? What had happened? He had been running one minute, and the next he was lying in a pit, hurting all over.

Above him he saw a patch of blue across which a cloud drifted. This hole was really deep. He sat up and cautiously felt for broken bones. He seemed to be in one piece, but his neck was stiff, as if he'd had a whiplash.

He staggered to his feet and saw with dismay that the opening of the pit was some feet above his head, its sides hard-caked and as smooth as con-crete. How was he going to get out? He put a bare foot on the side of the pit and dropped it again. Nothing there to give him any leverage.

This was really something. He sat down with his knees drawn up under his chin to think it out. He could yell for help, but when he tried it his voice sounded hollow, stifled. He'd be willing to bet it never got to the top of the hole.

Things looked dark, and Scotty's forehead creased in a scowl. Why do things like this always have to happen to me? Edward does stuff all the time that scares him silly, but he never gets into these jams.

His resentment against his lucky brother faded, however, as he remembered how respectfully Edward had treated him after he'd successfully climbed the mountain. And last night it was cold but he had slept soundly, only to find Edward's red jacket over him when he awoke this morning. He wished he could see his brother looking down at him right now. But who would be looking for him in a hole in the ground?

Time passed. He was tired and his mind was dull. A mosquito came into the hole singing noisily and dive-bombed at him. He clapped his hands over him and missed. If he had to spend the night down here the mosquitoes would finish him by morning. He pictured his remains, a pitiful little heap of bones and hair, without even his clothes to identify him.

The mosquito lost interest and took off, and Scotty leaned back and closed his eyes. No bright ideas came. When he opened them again they rested on the barely visible end of a root projecting from the hard earth opposite him. He looked at it indifferently, then sat upright, measuring the distance up to the root, and from the root to the top of the hole. If he could dig out the dirt around it, it might give him something to stand on, and from there—he'd try it.

He stood up and began to dig at the hard earth with his fingers. He hardly dented the surface at first, and even spat on it to soften it. But as he continued to prod, breaking his fingernails, he finally managed to pry away the surface dirt from around the stub. From then on it was easier. He was glad to see, as he worked, that the root was a tough one, sinewy and strong.

When he judged it was exposed sufficiently, he stood away and leaped at it with all his strength. He made it and clung to the projection with his bare toes, his palms flat on either side of the pit. Now for the real test.

He grabbed for the sod at the top and, straining until he thought his muscles would pop out of his skin, drew himself up—and out! He lay on the ground, panting like a thirsty pup in the hot sun.

Surprisingly, nothing had changed during his eternity in the pit. The stream murmured sleepily, and orange and black butterflies flitted over a patch of tiny star-shaped flowers. A breeze stirred the willows so that they bowed like gracious ladies, and the Oregon jays sassed each other in the brush. Leaning on his elbow, Scotty watched an insect crawl industriously up a blade of grass and then turn around and come down. Big deal.

He must have drowsed because he came to suddenly with the realization that he was scorching hot. Wow! He was on his way to being burned to a crisp in the hot sun, without a stitch on. He waded down the stream for his clothes and dressed quickly, squirming as the rough fabric scratched his sunburn.

He still had the bluffs to examine, but he was cautious about where he walked this time. As he hiked alongside the wall of cliff, he was amazed at how smooth and unbroken it was.

He continued upstream for a little distance, and his eyes did finally light on a deep cleft in the rock. He thought at first it was a cave, and couldn't have been less interested, but a second glance showed him it was merely an alcove, created by an overhang. Above this overhang of rock the wall was somewhat broken and niched.

Scotty eyed his discovery with a big grin. What would the others say when he went back to camp and told them there was a place to climb the bluff and get back on Tomahawk Trail?

He hoisted himself up onto the overhang, put his foot into a wide niche higher up, and pulled himself up. He'd climb up a little way and have a look, so he'd know what he was talking about.

It was easy. There was a toehold here, a handhold there, and he climbed steadily. At last he hung on one toe on a narrow ledge and looked up. There wasn't anything close. Could he make it to that tiny knob of rock and then spider out to that place off to the right?

He stretched and reached for the knob, but it came off in his hand, almost throwing him off balance. He clung. No, he couldn't reach the crack he'd had his eye on without something in between, and there didn't seem to be a thing to get hold of.

He looked down. Oops, better not do that. He'd had no idea he was so high. He groped below him with one foot, and then remembered he'd really humped himself to get a toe on the ledge. How would he get down if his legs didn't reach?

His arms were beginning to tire. He had to do something, for his shoulders still ached from the experience in the pit and he didn't know how long he could hold out. He recalled with a sickening sensation his brother's words in the cave: "Your skull would crack on the stones like an egg."

He clung to the rock like a small bug in the sweltering sun, his muscles quivering with exhaustion. He was not even conscious that the tears were streaking his dirty face as he whimpered a frantic prayer.

13

Rained Out

EDWARD HAD NEVER BEEN so baffled. There had been no sign of Scotty at the swamp, nothing of any interest there, in fact, except a white-blossomed plant about three feet tall which grew in profusion in the soggy soil. He pulled up a specimen, and upon finding that its rootstock was a tuber with a lot of fibrous roots, he pocketed it so that he would have it for Ron to examine.

He stood at the edge of the marsh, pondering, then turned upstream. He hadn't gone very far when something caught his eye. It was Scotty's cap, snagged on a branch which stuck up out of the water. He waded in and picked it up, squeezing out the water. The kid had apparently been picking berries; there were a couple of soggy ones caught under the band.

Why didn't I take my responsibility for him more

99

seriously? Mom had said years ago, when Scotty fell off the garage roof, that she knew she'd never raise him. Dad had laughed at her. "That's only because he's such a blunderbuss. He'll muddle through, you'll see—probably outlive all his peers." Maybe.

He went on. The ground grew rocky and barren as he neared the west end of the Nose, and the stream, where it came out of the bluffs, was narrow. If Scotty wasn't here, there was no place else to look.

It was then that he heard, across the stream, a whimpering sound that stopped him dead. A wounded animal? He crossed over in one leap, lifted his eyes and saw his brother. The boy was spread-eagled high on the bluff, and there was that in his attitude which told the whole story. How long had he been clinging there? And how could he help him? Edward's mouth was dry.

He moved noiselessly to the foot of the cliff and spoke naturally. "Hi, Scotty. I'm here and we'll get you down. No problem." (Oh, let me be telling the truth.)

"Edward! I can't reach the toehold. What'll I do?"

"Take it easy, I'll guide you. Now, keep your right toe in the crevice and stretch your other leg down as far as it'll go, and over to the left. Attaboy. To the left now, farther. Still farther. Yes you can, just another inch. There you are."

Foot by foot he directed the exhausted boy, until

at last Scotty was on the overhang and then, jumping down, sank in a huddle on the ground.

"I never thought I'd be chicken," he said in a choked voice after a while. "Climbing up didn't bug me," he snapped his fingers weakly, "but I sure weasled out trying to get down."

"No use to criticize yourself like that," Edward said briskly. "You negotiated the descent in admirable fashion with help from 'Tower Control.'" He added, "And I don't mean *me* when I say 'Tower Control.'"

Scotty fidgeted. "I know what you mean ... Only a birdbrain would have climbed up there," he added humbly.

Edward squinted up at the wall, bathed in gold and orange by the setting sun. Maybe. But Ron's legs were a lot longer and he was experienced. "Come on, let's bid farewell to Birdbrain Bluff for now."

"I don't know if I can walk. I ache all over."

"You'll sleep well tonight."

"Not with this sunburn," groaned Scotty, and tottered back to camp without enough energy left to recount the day's experiences.

He stuck to Edward like a shadow the next day, springing to attention when firewood was mentioned, replenishing the mattresses with fresh branches, and accompanying Edward to the swamp to gather what Ron assured them was Wapatoo.

"They raise acres of it in the Sacramento Valley—call them tule potatoes." Ron leaned on his crutches. "Bring back a lot of them, and we'll roast them in the pit."

"We'll catch some fish on our way back, too," Edward promised, and they did. He marveled at all the sources of food they were finding on the Squaw's Nose, food they wouldn't have recognized as edible without Ron's expertise.

"We could be up here the rest of the summer without starving," he assured Scotty.

"Sure," grumbled Scotty, shifting the load of tubers he carried in his open jacket, "but you have to work like crazy for every bite."

The next day there was a change in the weather, the sun uncertain, and the sky full of puffy rolling clouds. As Edward came back from the Ramparts, where a muffling gray fog blotted out both the nearby shoulder of the mountain and the distant canyon floor, he wondered uneasily what it would be like on the Nose when winter showed its teeth.

Camp was empty, for Scotty had gone to the woods for target practice, and even Ron had taken off. He threw a few sticks on the fire, zipped up his jacket, and sat down close to the blaze. Ron came back after a while, tossed down his crutches and lowered himself to a log.

"Still can't bear your weight on your ankle?" Edward asked.

Ron must have thought he was pushing him,

because he said shortly, "I'll let you know when I'm ready to climb."

The day passed, and it was a relief to have darkness come on early. Edward stretched out on his back and stared up at a watery moon, half hidden by ragged racing clouds. A wind had arisen, and it whipped up the fire with sudden gusts which briefly illuminated the trees and the bluffs so that they stood out like black cutouts.

Each night, with the vanishing of the sun, a new world sprang into being. When the silver stars sparkled in a dark blue sky and the moon looked down in soft radiance, God seemed near, and rescue from the mountain certain.

But tonight Edward was in a strange world, desolate, unfamiliar. The hump of the Nose looming above the meadow, the black-shadowed cliffs, the moving branches of the trees, all were grotesque, menacing. He thought longingly of home, and deliberately tore his thoughts away. He'd be blubbering like a baby in a minute. He wasn't praying hard enough, that was the trouble. It took faith, lots of faith, and he'd have to scrounge up enough so that God would hear his prayers.

He drifted at last into an uneasy sleep, to dream that he was once more outside Pirates' Cave while the lightning flashed and thunder shook the world. The hail pelted him and, looking up, he saw a tremendous rock toppling, about to crush him. He cried out, and sat up. It wasn't hail, but it was real

103

rain, and that was real lightning illuminating the sky with streamers of green light.

Another bad storm! The wind moaned in the treetops, and big drops hissed on the logs. They would be soaked to the bone, and the fire would splutter and smoke and go out.

As he wondered how the others could sleep through the growling thunder, Scotty flopped over, mumbling something, and Ron sat up. Thunder crashed and Scotty came wide awake. "Hey, I'm getting wet!" he exclaimed indignantly.

What to do? The woods were not safe in a storm. There was no shelter on the Nose.

14

Bad News

THEY HUDDLED CLOSE to the smoking fire, while the midnight drizzle rapidly increased to a cold, pelting rain.

"An experience such as this should not befall a canine," Edward complained, groping for his hat. As he slammed it onto his head, a sudden memory hit him. "Hey, Scotty, the overhang. How about the overhang at Birdbrain Bluff?"

"That little cave? Sure, let's go."

"Can you make it across the stream, Ron?" Edward asked as he grabbed the rucksack containing all their earthly possessions.

For answer, Ron leaned over the hissing fire and drew out a protruding branch to use as a torch. "You lead; I'll follow."

They dashed toward the stream.

"Watch out for deep holes," Scotty warned as they gained the other side.

They reached the overhang and crowded under.

"It's not the Hilton," Edward leaned out of the opening to shake his cap, "but it's a roof over our heads."

Although the rain was splashing down the face of the cliff and running over the stony ground toward the stream, the floor of their little refuge was dry.

Scotty managed to strut while remaining seated. "Ha! If it hadn't been for me you wouldn't have known about this place. I guess you couldn't get along without me, I'm the one that always— Hey, Ron," he broke off suddenly, "you made it over here without your crutches. Is your ankle better?"

"Right."

"Then you can climb the bluff tomorrow and we'll all be home in nothing flat." Scotty stretched out with a noisy yawn and fell asleep almost at once, although he'd never been able to sleep through an electrical storm at home.

Edward sat cross-legged on the uneven floor, a flood of relief washing over him at the realization that their ordeal was almost over. Why had he ever doubted that his prayers would be answered? Of course, the bluff would be no cinch to scale, but Ron could do it. The guy could do anything. He had brought them through this whole adventure without a mishap.

Ron was strong, his judgment good. He never

had much to say but he knew everything about the outdoors. Yes, Ron would climb the bluff and bring about their rescue.

It was time, he thought. They were fed up with scratching for a bare existence, thin, hungry and dirty. What was it Huck Finn's friend Jim had said when Huck had pointed out that "these things are adventures"? "I don't want no more adventures." Me either, Jim.

It was good to sit there safe from the storm which raged outside. Why had he thought the night menacing? There was a wild splendor about it. He sat gazing with awe at one of creation's spectacular shows, seeing how the fields and the woods flashed into vivid life each time the lightning stabbed the sky. The roar of the stream as it rushed between its banks under the tossing willows was like a powerful organ. Beneath the overhang they were like drowsy woods creatures snug in their holes while wind and rain battered at their door. It was like a scene from *The Wind in the Willows*.

After a while he said to the figure that sat so silently beside him, "Ron, of course you won't be doing any climbing on that ankle just yet. But how long do you figure it'll be?"

"What'll be?"

"Us—up here."

"Here, under the overhang?"

He could be maddening. "On the Squaw's Nose, Ron."

The other boy cleared his throat and then didn't speak after all.

"Of course, you haven't had a look at the bluffs yet." Since Ron was still silent, he went on, "Scotty climbed up the other day, but his legs were too short to reach some of the footholds."

Ron hunched himself closer to Edward, and again cleared his throat. "I was there today—yesterday, that is—examined the whole cliff from the marsh to the west end of the Nose."

"Yes?"

Ron moved restlessly. "No way, Ed."

Edward saw his face in a sudden flicker of lightning. So that's how it was.

"I know how you feel," Ron muttered.

"That's OK," Edward replied woodenly, hardly aware that he'd spoken.

"I felt as if I'd been kicked in the stomach. It couldn't be done without gear, old buddy."

"Shows what an ignorant slob I am for ever thinking it could."

"I hate to tell Tiger."

"We won't until we have to."

Edward felt terribly tired suddenly, washed up.

The rain was slashing down in sheets which formed a silver veil across the entrance of the recess. He listened to it drumming on the overhang and racing wildly down the slope. He wouldn't think of the future, he'd keep his mind on the present. What would this rain do to their camp?

The meadow would be like a wet sponge, the slippery grass squeaking underfoot, the tall weeds flattened to the ground. Their evergreen beds would be dripping; the fire would be out.

He raised his head from his hunched knees. "Could we survive a winter on the Nose?"

"I dunno."

"How's our supply of matches?"

"Fair. Rain doesn't necessarily put out a good strong fire. And I'm betting there'll be some live coals in our pit when this is over."

Edward had never seen it rain so hard. Would the swollen stream overflow its banks and creep up to their little refuge? Where could they go from here? He gave up any thought of the higher ground of the woods when a rending crash from that direction announced the falling of a tree. Well, it was stupid to worry about something you couldn't control.

He lay down close to Scotty and put an arm around him—for warmth, of course. He must have dozed off finally because when he opened his eyes again morning had come, drippy and gray. The rain had stopped but the stream was twice its normal size, and a dead fish lay on the bank.

"Some storm when even the fish drown," Scotty said.

They waded into the muddied brown waters of the stream and slithered up the oozy clay of the bank, where wet vines slapped them, sending showers of water down their necks. In the meadow, water lay in all the little hollows, and the long grass twined coldly around their ankles as they squelched toward camp.

Camp itself was a disaster area. The choking acrid smoke that drifted up from the blackened logs made their eyes smart. The stakes rigged to hold their cooking pot leaned crazily in the rain-softened earth, and their fir beds were soggy.

Edward knew the others felt like he did, chilled, hungry, muscle-sore from hours in cramped quarters. All he wanted was to get warm, eat his head off, and sleep like a polar bear. How would they ever get a fire going again?

Ron answered his unspoken question. "First thing to do is find a dead stub in the woods that's stump-dried. Rain doesn't penetrate dead wood after it has stood a while. Jack pine burns when it's green, and it's easy to chop. So is spruce. No problem. Let's go."

Scotty, squatting near the smoking embers, dashed a knuckle into his reddened eyes. "I'm h-hungry," he blurted, "and I don't wanta look for firewood or fish or pick berries or anything. I'm sick of camping, Ed." He ducked his head and wiped his nose on his sleeve.

"Aren't we all," Edward agreed, not looking at him. "From present indications, however, I'd predict that we will be affixed to the Squaw's Nose as firmly as a wart for a few days, so we might as well make ourselves comfortable for the duration."

"This isn't fun anymore."

"Know what we'd be doing in Cleveland this sweltering July day, Scotty?"

Scotty pondered. "Ugh! Taking the pop bottles into the supermarket for a refund, or cleaning out the garage. Hurry up, let's get our fire started." He jumped to his feet.

They salvaged enough live coals from the pit to start a fire—they were guarding their matches— and though Ron warned that fishing wouldn't be good until the creek lowered, roots lifted easily out of the rain-soaked earth.

Edward moved through the hours of the day, doing his share of the chores, kidding with Scotty, showing an interest in getting their camp back into shape, but underneath it all he felt absolutely numb.

A watery sun appeared in midafternoon, too late to dry out their beds, but Ron predicted the next day would be warm and bright. "There's something we've got to do tomorrow that we should have done before this."

"Yup, you're going to climb the cliff." Scotty, feeling better by this time, danced on his toes and jabbed his fists at Ron.

Ron was silent. What did he have in mind?

15

Food from the Sky

SCOTTY OBJECTED STRENUOUSLY when Ron proposed building a brush shelter. "That's a lot of work when we're only going to be here a couple of more days."

He looked sick when Edward told him the truth. "On the level? Ron can't make it to the top of the bluff?" After mulling over the facts for a few minutes, he said gruffly, "So what? I can take it if you guys can."

Ron said, "A brush hut will be protection from wind and rain—light rain, anyway, and sun, too."

Scotty was immediately intrigued as Ron lashed a crossbar to the trunks of two pines. He showed them how to fasten poles to this bar about a foot apart, slanting them and pressing the sharpened ends firmly into the ground.

The next step was to weave flexible branches as

crossbars through these poles, thus forming the framework of a lean-to. In the meantime, Scotty was put to work collecting long grass to use as thatch, which was tied into bundles with tough vines. When enough of these were thickly overlaid on the skeleton of the shelter, the result was as good protection from the weather as a tent would provide.

Edward was secretly proud of the way Scotty stuck to the job, not once wandering off on his own pursuits. He had dropped his excess weight, and what he had lost in pudginess he had gained in firm muscle. They were all browner and harder than the day they had started up Tomahawk Trail, though naturally they looked like scarecrows.

Edward sat back on his heels now and eyed their dwelling. "Now let the hurricane roar."

He hoped his enthusiasm didn't sound forced. Actually, he was puzzled and discouraged by their situation. He had done a lot of serious thinking since they'd landed on the Nose and had just begun to see God's hand in it all. God drew people to Himself through trial and difficulty, and He had put them into this frightening situation to teach them to pray and depend on Him. It made sense. Edward had noticed that each time when they'd thought the jig was up, God had delivered them. They'd gotten out of Pirates' Cave but found themselves still trapped. Then God had gotten them out of the Throne Room. Now that they were trapped on the Nose, He'd again showed His care by providing food and water.

All of this had built up his faith, made him see how important prayer was. Made him ashamed, too, of the way he'd neglected God when he thought he didn't need Him. And now, just when he was getting someplace, when he'd scraped up all the faith he could muster and was expecting a miracle, the bottom had dropped out. The bluffs were unscalable.

Maybe none of those rescues was God's doing after all. Maybe it was happenstance they hadn't been killed in the earthquake, that he had climbed that wall successfully and shoved the tree in so the others could get out. It wasn't unusual for streams to flow across mountain meadows, and unless you were in a barren desert there was bound to be plant life to keep you alive.

But it didn't quite jell—too many coincidences. It had to be God. But if so, why had He failed them now? For this was the end. He hadn't prayed hard enough, that had to be the answer. He had to have more faith. But how to get it? It was a strain even to put up a front for Scotty lately, to act as if everything was bound to turn out all right when he had no assurance they wouldn't all starve or die of exposure when winter came. If it depended on him and his puny faith, they were finished right now.

He needed to be alone to think things out. It was astonishing how much togetherness there was up

115

here on the mountain. A fellow had no time to commune with his soul. Like now, when he announced he was going down to the Fishbowl to try his luck, Scotty was immediately on his heels.

"I don't need the company of an elephant," Edward warned. But Scotty didn't know enough to take the hint.

Edward was relieved to see, as they reached the stream, that the muddy waters had cleared and swarms of insects were darting over the surface of the pool.

With a warning motion to Scotty, he stretched out prone on the bank, and lay motionless until he sighted a good-sized black-backed fish. Very quietly he slipped his hands into the water and lifted out the arching form. Scotty's mouth popped open as he laid it on the stones, but he closed it again at his brother's warning motion. Keeping his head in the shadows, Edward leaned over again. A small fish lay in a tangle of moss just beneath him.

"Will we ever eat tonight," Scotty exclaimed in a whisper as Edward laid the second fish on the bank.

An instant later something resembling the Polaris surfaced, a dazzle of orange-brown, and sailed by, scattering the small fry before him as the school bully scatters the third graders. Scotty's yell pierced Edward's eardrums and he jumped, and Scotty, who had been leaning over his shoulder, lost his balance and went headfirst into the pool. Edward sighed deeply.

"That was Grandpappy," he said as Scotty emerged.

The dripping boy shook his fist at the Fishbowl. "I'll get him yet. You wait and see."

Two fish and a few roots for three guys who hadn't had a bite all day. Depression settled on Edward. And then occurred one of those twists in their fortunes which he found so confusing.

They were skirting the woods on their way back to camp when Scotty, shivering in his wet clothes, pointed out the oak tree where the hawk lived. As Edward craned his neck, shading his eyes with one hand, a large bird rose out of the canyon and circled high above them.

"There he is now!" shrilled Scotty. "That's him, Ed. Look at that wingspread!"

"And there comes another one. Maybe it's his mate."

"Mate nothing. They're going to fight."

"What's the first one carrying in his talons?" They both stared, mystified.

The second hawk, though slightly smaller, came on in hot pursuit. He swooped, but his would-be victim dipped and beat upward. When directly overhead, circling, the aggressor came on again, screaming hoarsely. He struck, and feathers drifted down, and not only feathers, but something solid which plumped to the earth near the boys.

117

Both birds banked off and sailed screaming into the brush as Scotty picked up the limp object by the feet and held it out to him. It was a rabbit.

Edward, recalling a Bible story about a prophet being fed by the ravens, was too awed to speak.

16

Empty Hopes

EDWARD DRAGGED THE LOG up the slope to the bridge of the Nose. Now that the sun had burned off the swirling fog which hugged this area early in the day, it was time to build up the signal fires which had died down during the night. He fed the pair of fires with pine cones and twigs until the flames leaped up, then rolled the log onto them so that both ends would burn simultaneously. He knelt there, waiting until the log burned steadily, then added moss and green leaves to create a smudge. Only when both fires were sending up a pall of black smoke did he leave them.

Ron had been painfully blunt about the uselessness of smoke signals. "You're wasting your time, Ed." He sounded scornful. "Nobody'll see a wisp of smoke in all the fog that hangs over the Nose."

But the Nose wasn't always wrapped in fog, and

to the summer people at the beach the Squaw's Nose was a curiosity. They'd be looking up here a lot.

As for planes, Ron said indifferently, "Their routes don't take them over the Nose—too much fog."

Ron didn't waste his time thinking about the future. He had apparently given up any expectation of rescue and was concerned only in securing food for each day. He hadn't any luck catching fish with his bare hands, but he had added dandelion greens, cattails and watercress to their diet.

Edward stubbornly tended the signal fires daily, and had sacrificed his white T-shirt as a distress banner. It dangled, gray and tattered, from the top branches of a pine. Also, he and Scotty were carrying white stones from the base of Birdbrain Bluff to the slope, to form the giant letters SOS. They had laid out the S and O yesterday and today would complete the other S.

Meantime, Ron's sarcasm was no help. "You looking for the little green men to rescue us? No self-respecting pilot would fly low enough to see your signals."

Edward went doggedly ahead with the project anyway. "God knows all about the mess we're in," he told Ron, "and He'll do something about it. Just the same, He expects us to do our part."

He'd said very little to Ron about his faith, and the other boy received this comment just as he'd expected: with an uncomprehending stare. "You expect *God* to get us off the Nose?"

He looked away from the skepticism in Ron's dark eyes. "He answers prayer."

"Beats me," Ron said. "If there were really Somebody up there, I figure He wouldn't have let us get into this jam in the first place."

Scotty, listening, looked to his brother to stop the unbeliever's mouth, but Edward could only say lamely, "He has reasons we don't know about."

"Sure," Ron said politely.

So both Edward and God were on the spot. When they'd first discovered the meadow and the stream, Ron had talked of "Somebody up there" looking out for them, but now that their existence on the Nose had dragged on for nine days, according to the notches on Edward's calendar stick, Ron had given up on God.

"Well, I haven't," Edward muttered to himself as he started out on his rounds of the Nose. He was making periodic tours of inspection, in case anything should change below the ridge. Rocks could shift or split, break loose and roll, open up passages in the precipice which would make descent possible for them. Look at what the earthquake had done.

He hiked along, calling things to God's attention. "Look what You'd accomplish if You'd get us out of this. Ron would have to admit You answer prayer, Scotty would have more faith, and I could tell people later what You'd done for us—it would be a good thing for all of us."

As he came back to camp, Scotty yelled, "Get a move on! There's dessert for dinner."

He broke into a jog, and Scotty ushered him excitedly into the shelter. There, on the rough shelf Ron had contrived, stood the wooden bowl he had gouged out of a piece of log. Inside the bowl was a honeycomb—evidence that Ron had raided the bee tree near the Bathtub.

The honey was finger-lickin' good. When the bowl was empty Ron went to the marsh to replenish their supply of wapatoo and wild onions, and Edward and Scotty completed their SOS on the hillside.

Then, with no excuse for putting it off longer, Edward went slowly across the stream to the bluffs. If this idea that had gotten stuck in his mind was right, that Ron had simply turned chicken about the climb, he'd rather not know it, for it would force him—but that was unthinkable. He knew he wouldn't be satisfied, though, until he'd made his own appraisal.

A careful observation of the bluffs that afternoon both relieved and appalled him. "No way," Ron had said, and he was so right. Such toeholds as had lured Scotty were nonexistent higher up, the whole structure of the bluff changing and stretching upward from there like smooth gray glass.

Edward stood near the overhang with his arms

crossed, staring at that prison wall. He was more puzzled by this turn of events than he'd ever been. He'd prayed a lot and he'd done his best, like a lot of other people when they were in trouble. And it had all come to nothing.

But then, look at the martyrs. In spite of their faith they'd lost their lives. That didn't mean that God didn't care, though. What did it mean?

He roused himself after a while, crossed the stream, and was on the bank when he heard the sound. He didn't recognize it at first, that low rumble. Not thunder, oh no, not thunder. It grew to a roar, and his heart began to thump so hard he couldn't separate its clamor from the hum of the aircraft overhead. Then he was dashing across the meadow, cheering like a football fan. How could he have doubted God?

Ron appeared from inside the shelter, and Scotty came tearing out of the woods, waving his cap aloft.

In the dazzle of the sun the flying white bird sped on its inland course, heedlessly, unwaveringly. It appeared smaller and smaller as its drone slowly died away in the distance.

"Didn't even dip his wings," Ron said when the plane was only a silver flash in the empty sky. There was a mocking light in his eye.

"You didn't expect him to. You hoped he wouldn't, just to prove I was wrong," Edward said heatedly. "You and your negative attitude!"

"Attitudes don't change facts," Ron said with maddening calmness.

"I'm not so sure. Anyway, now that you've quit on us, you couldn't see a fact if it stood up and spit in your face."

Ron's eyes blazed. "Who're you calling a quitter?"

"What's your word for it?"

Ron's fist clenched. "What do you expect me to do, dive off the Nose? Grow a pair of wings and fly up the bluff?"

"Hey, you guys!"

They whirled toward Scotty, and their faces relaxed.

"Sorry, Ron. I don't know what made me sound off like that."

"That's OK, old buddy."

"Why is everybody just standing around?" Scotty demanded. "I'm hungry."

17

The Scorned Gift

THE DAYS DRAGGED BY and no other planes appeared. Was he wasting his time, Edward wondered, tending the signal fires day and night? They invariably needed replenishing when he was in a sweat to do something else, or so beat he could hardly lift a finger, let alone a load of heavy firewood.

He was alarmed, too, because the fish were growing suspicious and he had been unable to catch any for the last two days. The last thing he needed was a pool full of smart-aleck fish.

One night he lay awake listening to the patter of rain on the thatch—they were sleeping in the shelter because of showers. Today had been the two weeks' anniversary of their starting up Tomahawk Trail. He'd never get over trying to find an answer to why it had all ended like this. Was God telling him something that he couldn't hear? Had he been so indifferent to Him all his life that God couldn't get through to him now?

Maybe He's punishing me for choosing to hike up to the cave rather than attend the Bible conference with Mom. Oh, come off it, God doesn't go around getting even like some people do. Look how good He's been to us so far. But that makes it even more confusing. Why keep us alive now if we're going to die in the end anyway?

His eyes burned, staring into the dark. It would be better if I were more like Ron, he thought, if I'd stop searching for answers and live from one day to the next without thinking too much. What'll we eat tomorrow? That's more to the point.

At the first shimmer of dawn he slid off his bed. As he stooped at the opening of the shelter, his eye lighted on Scotty's jacket where he had flung it last night. The safety pin on the pocket flashed him a message, and he grinned suddenly. Would it work? He bent over and unfastened it, then groped in the pocket for Scotty's wad of cord. His old knife was there too.

In the willow thicket he found the straight pole he was looking for, peeled off the twigs, and tied a length of cord to it. He took a few minutes to twist the pin into the shape he wanted, and tie it on.

It was no great feat to catch a grasshopper, its wings heavy with dew, in the glistening meadow.

Under a sheltering branch, Edward slid his line

into the pool. Almost immediately a brown form darted at the bait. Man, how the fellow rushed to commit suicide. Seconds later he drew the fish out, leaping and flopping, and rebaited his hook. A safety pin had to be the greatest invention known to man.

In minutes he had another, then two more. With his improvised gear he might even catch Grandpappy, the insolent old tail-flirter. The thought was enough to keep him sitting there in the shade of the dipping willows until Scotty came down to the stream to wash.

His eyes bulged as he looked at Edward's hook and line. "Is that my safety pin? That pin may keep us from starving." He danced on his toes, jabbing his fists at an imaginary opponent. "You can thank me for those fish, Ed. I'm the one that brought that safety pin."

"And had this in mind when you did, no doubt?"

"Never you mind. That makes five for me, the hammer, my big lunch, the candles, the cord, and now my safety pin." He snickered. "Ron said you were probably down here tickling the fishes' bellies to make them roll over. Wait till I tell him you caught that mess with my pin."

"Run ahead and tell him in private. If I hear another word I'm liable to kill you."

"Can't take it, huh?" Scotty raced off, still chortling.

The day which had begun well did not stay that

127

way. Edward ripped out half the seat of his jeans on a log and came home, flapping and indignant. Why should such a thing happen to him? Scotty was the natural object for such a mishap to light upon.

Misfortune had also tapped Ron on the shoulder. He had tested an unfamiliar tuber and had broken out in hives which he was making a superhuman effort not to scratch.

Worst of all, when Edward and Ron returned from their busy morning in the woods and marsh, Scotty, who had been stationed at camp to keep the fire going, had let it go out while he was stalking a squirrel. He had then compounded his sin by wasting four matches trying to relight the fire, and the wapatoo buried earlier in the ashes was still raw and hard.

Hunger could sure make a fellow irritable.

"Look what I made for you, Ed." Scotty held up what vaguely resembled a spoon, a stick with one end whittled out to form a slight depression.

Edward looked up from the coals he was trying to blow into life. "What good is it? Give me something to use it on and I could be enthusiastic."

Scotty's face fell.

"Did you keep the signal fires burning?"

"Aw, go milk a rattlesnake," flared Scotty.

Edward plodded up the slope with an armful of dead branches. On the Nose, charred embers confronted him where the signal fires should have been sending up their wavering pillars of black smoke. These signals might never be noticed, he admitted to himself as he applied the burning branch he'd brought from the campfire to a pile of twigs and fir cones, but we can't take anything for granted. Someday somebody's going to look up here and wonder where that black smoke is coming from every day, always in the same place, never spreading. Aren't they? Not a chance, Ron said. But you couldn't trust the judgment of a guy who had given up. Hopelessness dulled your wits, killed your imagination.

He met Ron on the slope as he returned to camp.

"I'm going after some pine tree bark for Tiger," Ron said.

Edward looked blank.

"The inner bark is a good disinfectant bandage after you boil it to make it soft. That cut on his finger isn't healing and the medicine from the first-aid kit is used up now."

"What cut?"

"He sliced it trying to carve a spoon."

Edward hurried down the slope. As he skirted the campfire he half noticed the flames licking at a smooth stick on top of the logs. He gave it a second look. It was the spoon Scotty had worked on for him.

He went slowly toward the shelter. But Scotty wasn't there.

18

A Close Call

SCOTTY FELT LIKE A SENTRY sentenced to be shot for sleeping on duty. It wasn't anything Edward had said, exactly. He'd hardly said anything. But his brother could say more when he wasn't saying anything than anyone he knew.

There was only one way to make up for goofing, and that was to do something really neat—like catching Grandpappy. He got the pole and line from the shelter and started for the creek.

He hated having Edward think he was a dummy. It used to be Ron he wanted to impress, but more and more Ron and Edward were changing places in his mind. Edward didn't look like much, especially with the seat of his pants flapping! He didn't have big shoulders like Ron, and he was skinny and his muscles didn't bulge.

Mom would have been glad to hear what he'd

said about having faith in God. Ron thought stuff like that was for the birds. There was a lot Ron didn't know.

It was a relief to escape from the burning afternoon sun into the shade of the creek bank. He poked around until he found a fat white grub in a rotting stump, and baited his hook. Remembering Edward's advice, he got out of sight behind the bushes and dropped his line into the water as gently as you'd lay a sleeping puppy in its basket.

He didn't stay hidden long, for there was a tug on his line, and he popped his head over the bank to see what was going on. Great! In minutes he was laying a flopping brown fish on the bank behind him. At this time of day, too! Edward claimed the only time to fish was early morning or when the sun was setting.

He rebaited his hook and prowled along the bank trying to spot his prey. He didn't see him in the white ripples under the little waterfall, but he soon caught another good-sized fellow there. He should be happy with these two, for they had to weigh three pounds apiece, but he wasn't about to be satisfied with anything less than the king of the Fishbowl. Where was the old fellow hiding out, anyway?

He stretched out near the pool and lay motionless. A dragonfly perched on an overhanging branch, wings outspread like a fairy godmother. The drone of insects in the thicket made him sleepy. Fishing could be kind of dull. Yawning, he leaned over the bank.

At once his heart began to pound. The king was there, under the overhang of the bank, lying in a mass of sodden leaves and moss. Oh, he was super, a yard long and a beautiful orange-brown with flashes of red.

He doesn't know I'm within a mile of him. Shall I slip my hand in and lift him out? Better not; he's faster than a guided missile. I'll dangle my bait in front of him and make him drool.

He dropped his line into the pool, where it drifted, then settled. There was a stir in the water, and the big trout struck. The battle was on. Grandpappy rose, flailed with terrific strength, turned and fled. Scotty, on his feet now, played him, giving him line, drawing him in, in a fever lest the safety pin wouldn't hold or his line break.

Grandpappy had a fighting heart and the strength of an ox. He jumped again and again, and tore across the pool and back to rid himself of the hateful hook. Scotty was unaware of the salty sweat rolling down his upper lip into his mouth.

At last he drew the great fish in and held the exhausted creature in his hands. He surveyed his trophy almost with reverence, and stroked him caressingly. Oh, you beauty, what a fight you put up! And I was the one to land you. Edward's been trying and trying, but it was me.

No telling how long this fellow had been the king

of the stream, speeding and darting back and forth, flashing out of the water for bugs, lying on the stones or taking a nap in his hole under the bank, free as air.

His hand slowed its stroking. Oh, come on! Was he out of his mind? It was no use. He could no more fry and eat Grandpappy than he could his cocker spaniel, Ginger. With tears in his eyes Scotty drew the hook out of the great fish's mouth and slid him into the water.

The trout lay motionless for a few seconds, then swam tentatively across the pool. Suddenly he streaked back to his hiding place in the leaves. Scotty clapped his heels together and saluted. "Mum's the word, Grandpappy."

His catch in his cap, he waded downstream toward the swamp, for he wasn't ready yet to face the others. There were some large cattails, he saw, halfway around the swamp. They'd be mighty good with his fish, for the tubers tasted like baked potatoes when they were roasted in the pit. He hadn't taken half a dozen steps, however, when he found himself struggling in the thick mud. One foot went down deep, and when he tried to pull it out, the swamp clutched at it frighteningly. The harder he worked to extricate himself, the worse it was.

Quicksand! You weren't supposed to struggle in quicksand. Stand still, then.

Motionless, his breath sticking in his throat, he

looked around. Nothing to be scared about, Scotty old boy, there's solid ground right behind you. Take it easy, it's only your right leg that's gone in deep.

He never knew afterward how he managed it, but forcing himself to be deliberate, he drew himself out of the treacherous bog and got back on hard ground.

Whew, I'll never go near that spot again! Funny, it isn't like that where the wapatoo grows. He spat disgustedly. No one else ever got into the spots he did. Now he'd have to take a bath before he went back to camp. Big deal.

First of all, though, he'd climb the oak tree again. He hadn't had a chance to look around from up there the other day, with the hawk taking after him.

He laid his fish and gear at the foot of the tree and shinnied up the trunk, keeping a wary eye out for the yellow-eyed bird. Hawks had telescopic eyes and were hard to fool. He found a strong, heavy limb to sit on where he could look out over the fir-clad peaks and the brushy canyons.

He gazed down at the swamp and spied Edward, rucksack in hand, standing at the very point where he, Scotty, had just had his frightening encounter. He was going to wade into the quicksand!

Scotty leaned down. "Edward!" he yelled hoarsely.

His brother didn't turn his head.

"Get back! Keep away!" he shouted again.

There was no sign that Edward heard him. He leaned far out on the limb to get his attention, lost his hold and went crashing down. He hit the hard earth with a thud, and everything went black.

19

Edward's Treasure

EDWARD CHANGED HIS POSITION, stretching his cramped limbs without taking his eyes off Scotty's face. It looked blue, and his hands were cold to the touch, although on this warm August day he was wrapped in a sweater and three jackets.

The afternoon's happenings were a blur in his mind: the thud as Scotty crashed to the ground, the race to the stream for water to bring him back to consciousness, the dash across the meadow to summon Ron. When it was pretty certain Scotty had no broken bones, they had carried him to the shelter and doctored his bleeding knee and skinned elbow with the pine bark Ron had prepared earlier.

Scotty had been lying there ever since with closed eyes, only half conscious. He muttered the same words every now and then in a weak voice:

"Keep away, Edward." He was evidently delirious.

Ron came into the shelter. "I'm warming some stones in the fire. We've got to keep him warm."

Scotty opened his eyes. "Thirsty," he murmured.

Edward raised his head and held the wooden bowl to his lips. "How do you feel, bud?"

"All right." His eyes closed again.

All right. That's what he'd said when he broke his leg, and what he said when that big bully in the next block had knocked him down. He'd say it on his deathbed. Edward swallowed.

"What do you think, Ron?"

Ron cleared his throat. "Keep him quiet and warm, that's all I know to do for a concussion."

When morning came Scotty seemed no better. Ron joined Edward in the shelter. "How is he?" He leaned over and clasped Scotty's wrist. "Has he talked to you at all?"

"A little."

"Good. As long as he isn't out of his head—yup, he'll probably be a lot better today."

You don't really think so. You think it's all up with him.

"He's not like me, Ron. He's husky."

"Sure." Ron released Scotty's wrist. "I guess you're still—you know—expecting a miracle?"

Edward hesitated.

The look that passed over the other boy's face was gone before he could analyze it. Disappointment? Contempt?

He thinks I've lost my faith, but I haven't. It isn't that at all. I can hardly explain it to myself, so how can I make him understand? I don't know myself when my thinking changed.

As late as yesterday he had still been demanding that God get them off the Nose and not let them die up here. What had come over him? He was as sure as ever this morning that God loved them and cared about what was happening to them, but he was no longer insisting on his own way.

"I'll be down at the swamp." Ron turned on his heel.

Scotty opened his eyes. "Edward? You okay? I was afraid—the quicksand—" His voice trailed off and he closed his eyes again.

Quicksand? It all came clear in a flash. Edward heard again that warning shout and the thud, saw Scotty on the ground. He had been trying to warn him of danger. If his attention had been on himself he wouldn't have slipped, wouldn't be lying here now.

Edward cried.

When Ron came back they moved the patient out into the sunshine. Afterward Edward trudged up to Heartbreak Ridge to replenish the signal fires. He squatted on his heels near the flames, trying to bring his thoughts into order.

I don't know where to go from here, Lord. Do You want him to die? Talk to me!

If he expected a voice out of the blue or some

139

great revelation to burst on him, he was disappointed. He sat on, his hands clasped around his knees and his head bowed over them.

Lord Jesus, You're my Savior and I belong to You. But I'm not up to begging for my own way anymore, not even where Scotty is concerned. Sure, I wanted us to be rescued. I wanted to go home to Mom and Dad. But You love us and You know best, so I'm leaving it all in Your hands. Whatever You want is OK with me.

Would God think it was a copout? It wasn't. He'd gotten a lot of comfort out of those talks he'd been having with Him. He wouldn't want those to come to an end, for it had brought them so close together. But he was at the place where he wanted God to take over. It made sense.

He stood up, expecting to feel guilty now that he'd thrown the whole job onto Him, but instead he was conscious of an unexplainable lightness of heart as he went back to camp. He found Ron splitting some fish he had caught and lashing them to branches which he propped near the fire. Scotty was awake and watching the operation with languid interest.

As day followed day, the sense of Christ's approval wove itself into everything Edward did. It was exciting, this discovery he had made. God wasn't fed up with him, hadn't withdrawn in disgust because he had given up and asked Him to do as He pleased.

Nothing in the picture was changed. The old routine spun itself out one day and was inevitably resumed the next. Camp chores couldn't be neglected; the anxiety over Scotty continued. No, nothing was changed, and yet everything was. He wished he could share this new awareness with Ron, but he didn't know how. It didn't sound like anything much when you put it into words. Maybe later—

"I'm OK," Scotty always answered to questions about his condition. "You guys don't have to wait on me."

"Could you be a little more of a stinker, bud?" Edward complained. "All this sweetness and light makes me think there's a stranger in camp."

Scotty grinned a little. "I'll be my old repulsive self as soon as my head stops aching, scout's honor."

It really got to Edward. He picked up Scotty's slingshot as an excuse to get away, and wandered across the meadow. *Not that I could hit the broad side of a barn, even if there was any game up here to aim at.*

If they'd been lost on the mountain proper, there might have been rabbits, deer, perhaps even a cougar—perish the thought. Fortunately, there wasn't so much as a snake in their paradise on the Nose, no rattlesnakes, at least. The elevation was too high for them.

He selected some pebbles and went into the

woods, where a squirrel chattered impudently from a stump. He'd read that squirrel stew was a dish for a king, but as badly as they needed food he wouldn't want to kill the little fellow.

The next day, according to his calendar, was Sunday. Would Mom and Dad be in church? Wherever they were, the God he loved and trusted would give them the strength they needed.

Scotty was feeling better this morning. "I'm getting up," he announced as Edward returned from the stream with a pail of water. "Is there anything in the pit? I'm hungry."

"That's our Tiger," Ron said cheerfully. "It so happens—" He never finished his sentence, for they all heard the sound at the same time. That choppy rhythm was unmistakable.

They stood staring stupidly as the helicopter lifted slowly over the Nose. It circled overhead, and as Edward realized it was preparing to land in the meadow, the tears rained suddenly down his face. He ran, then, the water in the pail sloshing over his leg.

The chopper lowered, and when he recognized his father sitting beside the pilot, he sobbed aloud.

The signal fires had been sighted from the beach, Dad said, and had given them fresh hope when search parties had failed to find the trio on the other side of the mountain.

"When we noticed that they were always burn-

142

ing in the same place, never spreading or dying out, we got the message." There were dark circles around Edward's mother's eyes.

"You can imagine our excitement," his father said later as they were seated around Scotty's bed in the hospital. "We'd given up any idea of finding you alive in the cave when we saw the upheaval the earthquake had caused around the mouth. It'll take weeks to clear away that rockfall."

"Oh, don't talk about that awful earthquake," cried Edward's mother. "I never want to hear the word 'cave' again, either."

Scotty bounced upright. "But we've got to go back up there, Mom. We haven't found the treasure yet."

Hadn't they? thought Edward. He'd tell Mom and Dad all about it later. She wouldn't turn pale at the word "earthquake" when she learned that he'd never have found his own unique treasure without it.